CAMP SLAUGHTER

SERGIO GOMEZ

Cover design by: Teddi Black
Interior design by: Megan McCullough

For Derrick, who has been there for me since the beginning.

"It seems to me most strange that men should fear, seeing that death, a necessary end, will come when it will come"
–William Shakespeare, *Julius Caesar*

PROLOGUE

A NERVOUSNESS WAS WORKING itself into Nadine Lang's stomach as they drove deeper and deeper into the woods. It had been growing ever since they turned off the main highway and started down these narrow dirt roads between densely packed trees that seemed to never end. Everything around them was getting more lush and greener by the minute, giving new definition to 'wilderness' for folks like her and her husband.

Maybe I should've searched for 'second most secluded cabin,' Nadine thought. A weak smile formed on her face, but she was only half joking.

Her husband must have been just as unsettled, because he was driving faster now, as if in a hurry to get to the cabin. The road they were on was nothing more than a layer of pebbles between the trees to show drivers where they should go. If a car came from the other way, one of them would have to back up until they found a place to pull over to let the other one pass. At the speed Stephen was pushing the Rav4, Nadine wasn't so sure they wouldn't slide into the trees first, though. Especially around all of these curves.

"Stephen, maybe you should slow down?" Nadine said.

She saw her husband's face flush red as he grimaced. It was a facial expression she was very familiar with nowadays. *Nagging Nadine.* That was what her first serious boyfriend in college used to called her, and even several relationships and a marriage later it stuck in her mind. Nadine shrunk in her seat.

Stephen took in a deep breath, then said, "Sorry. Just hungry and tired."

He'd driven the entirety of their trip, with only one stop in the afternoon in which they filled up the vehicle with gas and filled their stomachs with greasy cheeseburgers that tasted like cardboard. But he recognized that she was right. He was driving too fast. Stephen let his foot off the pedal, and let the SUV drop down to a comfortable thirty miles per hour.

"I'm ready to get there already," he said, looking over at her with a weak smile on his face.

"Me too," she said, picking up the directions that were on her lap.

According to the Google Maps printout, they were only thirty minutes from Lakewood Cabin. With the moment of truth coming, she hoped more than ever that it would look like the pictures on the website. But really, what she was hoping for was that the place would somehow fix the problems between her and her husband and save their marriage from falling apart altogether.

Her mind turned to the surprise lingerie she had bought specially for this trip…the outfit she had hung all her hopes on to be spicy enough to reignite their passion for each other. It was a silly and farfetched idea, but all she had was hope.

The SUV stopped at the top of Lakewood Cabin's driveway. A squirrel running across the porch banister froze, identified where the foreign sounds were coming from, then scurried up a column and over the front awning before disappearing across the roof.

"Wow," Nadine remarked, admiring the beauty of the massive cabin before them.

Next to her, Stephen was already getting out of the car. Without taking her eyes off the cabin, she unlocked her door and stepped out. The gravel crunched underneath her sneakers, and it was so quiet out here that the sound echoed through the trees.

This place was even better than she'd hoped. Better than the website made it out to be, too, because the pictures online couldn't capture the sweet scent of cedarwood the summer breeze carried through the air.

Lakewood Cabin stood two stories tall, made entirely of logs. At the front of it was a deck large enough for a picnic table on one side and a porch swing on the other. An awning made entirely of wood protected the furniture from the elements of the weather.

Around the perimeter of the cabin were bushes with plump berries that were too vibrantly colored to be anything other than poisonous. Further out from the porch, in what could have been considered the "front yard," there was a pit for campfires with a metal barrel that held skewers and utensils for roasting.

Large trees with nuts and fruits growing on them towered over the cabin in a semi-circle, making it feel like Lakewood Cabin existed in a pocket isolated from the rest of the woods. It was the perfect private place for an author to retreat into to finish their latest manuscript, or that a family would rent out to get away from suburban life for a week of summer leisure.

Nadine was thinking about those steamy romance novels she'd started reading a few years ago, when things between her and Stephen went cold in the bedroom. A common theme in those books was for the protagonist and her lover to go into a cabin deep in the woods to have passionate sex, and Lakewood Cabin was exactly what she imagined when reading those scenes.

"Oh, Stephen! Stephen, isn't this wonderful!" Nadine walked around to the front of the SUV to see what her husband's reaction was, but he wasn't on his side of the car anymore. He was at the back of the vehicle, unloading, and hadn't heard a word she said.

"Nadine, can you get the door for me, please?" he said, coming up the driveway toward her carrying a cooler.

"Yeah," Nadine said, feeling the magic of the moment deflating because he hadn't even bothered to take in the sight for a second.

One of the reasons they'd come out here was for him to be away from work, but here he was, doing some form of work anyway.

Nadine trotted to get ahead of him. She took the keys from her purse and opened the cabin door. An expansive, rustic interior dominated by a fireplace taking up almost an entire wall greeted her. The place was somehow larger than the outside suggested it would be. Several antique-style lamps with dark green shades were placed around the main room, breaking up the monotony of the wooden walls and floors. On one wall hung an elk's head with great big horns and dark eyes that were eternally staring at nothing. If there was ever a place to kick back, drink some tea, and read a novel, it was here.

"This is quite the place," Stephen said, coming up behind her with the cooler.

"Isn't it marvelous?" Nadine said, shaking her head in disbelief. She was sure this was some dream, that she'd fallen asleep watching the trees rush past the window, and she'd wake up still in the SUV any minute now.

Of course, that didn't happen.

"Good pick," Stephen said, setting the cooler down.

Nadine looked over at him, and he looked back at her. For a second, she thought he was going to kiss her, but he didn't. He just blinked and turned away.

"Let's unpack some, then you can cook us up some sausages," he said, heading out the cabin.

"Okay," Nadine said.

Her voice was meeker in the expanse of the cabin. She didn't think it was possible, considering the lie behind the word when she was using it with him. 'Okay.' Everything was always 'okay'—even though it wasn't.

But here she was, in the middle of this large rustic cabin, finding out it was possible for her to sound meeker.

After unpacking and eating sausages in potato rolls slathered with mustard and topped with sauerkraut, Nadine and Stephen Lang went into the master bedroom. The room kept the same decorative theme as downstairs, a rustic, cozy place to rest. There had even been a buck's head hanging over the bed frame, which Nadine took the liberty of storing away in one of the closets. Stephen had laughed at her for that, and it felt good that she could still bring some joy to him.

Nadine changed into her lingerie while Stephen stripped down to his boxer briefs, then they both crawled underneath the covers. The room must have had good airflow or something, because despite the eighty-degree weather outside, it was chilly in here. Almost like autumn. The sheets felt cool against their skin when they moved under them to a spot that hadn't been touched for a good while.

They'd been cuddling in silence for a good thirty minutes now, but it hadn't turned into anything else. Nadine had her head against his chest and was playing with the salt-and-pepper chest hairs with an index finger, while Stephen had his arms around her. Even though they weren't speaking, neither of them knowing what to say, it felt good to finally have her husband's attention all to herself. No cell phone, no laptop, no television. Just them two lying in bed together.

For a moment it seemed like before, back when they were younger, back before Stephen's company had expanded to the size it was. Before the silent dinners together and the empty I-love-you's before bed.

Stephen was a partner for a digital marketing company that had clients all over the world, and in the last few years their clientele had exploded. The company started taking in jobs from Sweden, India, Russia, and so on, which meant dealing with each and every time zone around the globe. Some nights he'd have to stay up until four AM on a conference call with clients from Japan or Malaysia, and then have to wake up at seven AM to make a call to someone out in London. There was no set schedule to his work, so he was always connected and busy with no time for anything else.

The money was nice, but the life had started to drive a wedge between him and Nadine, and he knew this, but he couldn't pull himself away from it. He believed that at a certain point he would make enough money to make up for the emotional neglect, but the more money he brought in, the further he moved the goalpost.

When he first had that thought, he realized he was an apple that hadn't fallen far from the tree. Being the son of a restaurant owner, he knew a thing or two about being on the receiving end of emotional neglect from a loved one—but he still couldn't pull himself away from work. And it was that guilt of knowing he was no better than his father that made him agree to this getaway in the woods. This was his attempt at compromise, at reconciliation.

Now that he was away from work and lying in bed with her in this quiet cabin, the guilt was crushing him worse than ever. He stared up at the ceiling fan, watching the wooden blades spin around to try to distract himself from the ill feelings, but it didn't work.

It was his fault they'd gotten to this point, to the point where they needed some elaborate trip as a last-ditch effort before the big D word would enter the conversation. He kissed the top of Nadine's head and rubbed her back between the shoulder blades. It was as close as he would come to admitting he fucked up to her, because again, he was a fruit that hadn't fallen far from the tree. His father had never been one to apologize, either.

Nadine lifted her head up and kissed him on the lips. She tried to make it longer than a peck, and as much as he wanted to go along with it, the guilt settling in him was too much. He pulled away.

He felt like he would be cheating her out of the passion she was looking for if he forced himself into it, like he was paying someone with a counterfeit bill or something.

Stephen shook his head at her. "Not tonight, Nadine."

"Aw, come on Stephen," Nadine said, her eyes watering. "I thought the whole point of this trip was for us to be…I don't know. Romantic, or something like that."

He would've laughed if he didn't feel so bad about everything. "I just drove nearly seven hours, Nadine."

She sighed and slumped back down onto his chest. The truth was, she wasn't in the mood either. The lacey lingerie didn't even make her feel sexy. It was doing the opposite, actually. She felt like she was wearing something meant for someone younger than her, someone with a better figure. She thought about getting up to change back into regular underwear, but decided it wasn't worth disrupting the moment. Because in the back of her mind, she feared this would be the last time they ever did this.

"We haven't decided how long we'll be in Hawaii next month." Stephen said, hoping that a change of topic would bring her spirits back up—and his, too, for that matter.

"We haven't," Nadine said. "Have you thought about it?"

Next month, their eldest son was getting married. It was a destination wedding at the Big Island, and Nadine knew this was a bother to Stephen because it meant being away from work again. It was surprising to her that he'd agreed to this trip so close to the date of the wedding.

"I was thinking no more than a week," Stephen said.

"A week. Sure. That sounds fine to me."

They both went quiet after that. Stephen continued to watch the wooden fan blades spinning on the ceiling. Nadine rested her palm against his right pec and listened to his heartbeats.

Outside, the sun was almost below the horizon as day gave way to twilight. The moon could just be seen as a washed-out crescent against the purple sky. Early-to-rise crickets were chirping in the bushes, singing so loud it traveled up to the master bedroom and filled the silence between Nadine and Stephen.

However, the silence was starting to become uncomfortable. Nadine stirred under the covers to rustle them, for no reason other than to make noise. She opened her mouth to bring up Hawaii again, but froze when she heard a loud bang.

The sound came from downstairs, and through the open window at the same time. It was something from the front of the cabin. Some unknown thing in the middle of these empty woods.

Nadine felt Stephen's heartbeats kick. She looked up at him, seeing the same fear that tingled along her spine.

"Wh-what was that?" Nadine whispered.

He shook his head. "I don't know."

Another bang.

The wind. Maybe it was the wind. Maybe they'd left the front door open and the wind was banging it against the frame. Or maybe it was the screen door. It did look a little crooked, now that she thought about it.

Nadine moved off him and Stephen got up. She started to get up out of the bed with him, but he put an arm around her waist. "Stop. Stay here. It's probably nothing but I'll go and make sure, just in case."

"Okay, but come right back. Otherwise I'm coming to find you."

"Yeah," he said.

He stopped at the door and grabbed a broom leaning against the wall. It was something the landlord left as a message to renters to remember to clean up before leaving.

Stephen turned to her, shrugged, and gave her a thin smile. "If it's a racoon, I'll need something to beat him out with."

Nadine returned the smile, but it felt thin.

He left the room.

Nadine saw the hallway light come on. She drew up the covers close to her body, and waited for her husband to come back, straining to hear anything moving outside.

If they were anywhere other than the middle of fucking nowhere, he wouldn't have let his imagination run as wild as it was as he climbed down the stairs.

The first floor of the cabin wasn't even that dark, it was more like everything had taken on a purple hue rather than black darkness. But in the back of his mind was the fact that he and Nadine were likely the only people within miles of this place.

I shouldn't have agreed to this damn trip, he thought, but then another wave of guilt crashed into him. He'd been a bad husband. A terrible husband, actually. He had no basis to complain about his wife's attempt to save their marriage. Stephen let these guilt-ridden thoughts take over his mind. In some ways they were better than the uncertainty of what he would find out downstairs. The guilt he was at least familiar with.

He reached the bottom of the stairs and flipped a switch on the wall. The old-fashioned lamps flooded the living room with light. He saw the front door was closed tight.

Lights on. Door closed. He got his bearings back.

What he'd said to Nadine before leaving the room was probably right, it might've been a racoon or some other animal trying to get in.

Hopefully nothing bigger than that, he thought, relaxing. He loosened his grip on the broomstick.

Now that he was back to normal, he noticed his mouth was dry. He figured he may as well grab some refreshments while he was down here and started for the kitchen.

He went down the short corridor, made the bend around the wall that put him in the kitchen doorway…and stopped when he saw the refrigerator was open. Light spilled out, revealing someone standing in front of it, partially blocked by the fridge door and partially hidden in the shadows.

His toes went cold. No else should be here except him and his wife.

"H-hello, can I help you?" he asked. Maybe it was the landlord. Maybe someone else was renting a cabin up here and got the wrong place. Yeah. That must be it.

"Hello?" Stephen asked again, louder this time. Thinking the person might not have heard him over the noise of them clattering around the beer cans and foodstuffs they'd stocked in from the cooler.

The rummaging stopped, and the unexpected visitor froze. Stephen had been reaching for the light switch on the wall, but now he froze too, fear creeping in as he waited for what this intruder would do next.

For a few breaths, neither moved.

Then, the man rose up, holding the fridge door open, still lost in the shadows.

"*Hello!*"

"Uh… Yeah. I'm sorry, but you can't…can I help you? Who are you?"

"Shh," the person—a man—said to him, raising a finger to his lips.

Stephen threw his hand out to the wall, slapping the light switch on.

What he saw twisted his stomach in knots.

The guy's face was dry and cracked. Patches of it were peeling off like old wallpaper. The eyes, dark as obsidian, were set too far back into their sockets.

With his next breath he realized that it wasn't the man's face he was looking at. No, no. It was *a* face, but a face over a face. A mask. One that looked like it was made from actual flesh. No matter how he much he tried he couldn't shake the idea that this intruder into their cabin was wearing someone else's skin.

The room started to spin. Stephen reached out for the wall to keep himself from falling.

"Who are you?!" the man screeched, mockingly echoing Stephen's own question to him.

His voice was high-pitched, childlike, so unexpected coming from a man that tall and wide. He was built like a pro-wrestler, but the voice could have belonged to a Looney Tunes character.

The masked man reached behind him and when his arm came back up, he was holding a double-headed ax. It shone oddly underneath the ceiling lights. Stephen was transfixed by the metal blade. It shouldn't be here. This man shouldn't be here. None of this should be happening…

With a two-handed grip the man brought the ax up high over his head. He took a giant step forward and brought the ax down in a tight arc.

The blade went through the top of Stephen's head, splitting his skull in half down to the bridge of his nose. There was time for one passing thought that he should have let his wife screw him one last time…and then his dead body fell backward with the weapon still lodged in the head.

The masked man crouched down and tugged on the ax handle. It was lodged in there good, so he jiggled it around to a series of pops as the blade broke through the skull on its exit. Blood and brain matter slimed out of the top of Stephen Lang's head in a puddle of goo.

The man stepped through it as he started for the stairs.

Stephen was taking too long. She wasn't sure how many seconds had passed and the clock in this room was stuck flashing twelve o'clock, but she knew it had been too long.

Nadine pushed the covers off and got out of the bed. Without taking her eyes off the doorway, hoping Stephen would come through it any moment, she found her slippers on the floor and put them on. Now she really was wishing she'd changed into her pajamas. Going off to confront the unknown in a slinky thong and peek-a-boo bra didn't make much sense. It was so cold in the room now that her hands felt numb.

Stephen hadn't come back with some story about chipmunks on the porch. He was still downstairs, which meant something must be wrong.

She took in a deep breath and went out of the room.

Because of the lack of windows, it was quieter in the hallway than in the bedroom. Here, she couldn't hear leaves rustling or the crickets chirping outside. It made her feel isolated, and suddenly, the quietness was suffocating.

Nadine licked her lips and called out, "Stephen! Is everything okay?"

No response.

Of course not, the cabin was sturdy and solid, so much so that voices didn't seem to travel through it well. Sounds crashed into the dense wooden walls and died there.

She cursed whoever had built it this way as she walked down the hallway. At the top of the stairs she tried again. "Stephen? Can you hear me? Hello?"

Nadine was about to take her first step down, when someone that wasn't her husband came around one of the walls and stopped at the bottom of the stairs. He stared up at her with eyes that were too dark and a face that didn't move when he spoke, mockingly repeating her words back to her.

"'Teven! Hello! 'Teven! 'Teven!"

Nadine screamed, and ran.

Nadine slammed the bedroom door shut and threw the lock on, thinking that would be enough to keep him out.

Out in the hallway, the masked man lifted the ax to his shoulder, slick with blood and sharp on both ends. With a single heave, the head of the ax broke through and came out on Nadine's side. She screamed.

"*'Teven!*" the masked man mocked. *"Helllooo? 'Teven?"*

The ax head pulled back, tearing a hole in its wake, and a meaty hand came through in its place. *"Teven, is everything okay!?"*

She could hear him laughing out in the hallway.

Nadine bit back a scream and scanned the room for a weapon, anything, something, please God anything, but nothing stood out to her. The lamps? Maybe. But would they even do enough damage?

Screw it. She had to try something. And she could hide in the closet. Gain the element of surprise.

Yes, that was it.

She ran over to one of the lamps and picked it up, relieved to find out it was hefty. The power cord ripped right off the wall as she ran to the closet with it.

Meanwhile, the masked man's fingers felt around the doorknob for the lock like fat worms searching for food.

Nadine shut the closet door behind her, and a few seconds after that the masked man unlocked the bedroom door. He barged through, ax over his head, ready to strike.

But froze when he saw the room was empty. She was hiding.

"*Where are youuuu?*" He asked, lowering the ax and stepping through the room.

Inside the closet, Nadine held her breath while clutching onto the lamp.

She exhaled, as slowly and quietly as she could as she heard him hunkering toward her, his steps heavy against the wooden floor. She looked at the knob, but there was no lock. Of course not, it wouldn't make any sense for there to be.

She was going to be found, it was a forgone conclusion at this point. And he'd found her out quickly, too. How the hell had he done that?

It didn't matter. She readied the lamp.

A term she'd overheard once when Stephen was watching a football game popped into her head; Hail Mary. The phrase had stuck out to her because the religious overtone to the name seemed out of place with the rest of the sport. Here, in a life or death situation, the term was more fitting.

This was her Hail Mary moment.

The knob turned, and the door was flung open. Before her stood a gargantuan man, but even more frightening than his immensity was his hideous face. It was dry, bloated, and somehow too big for his head.

Without wasting another second, Nadine leapt forward and threw the lamp at him. The man got his arm up fast enough to protect his head and the lamp shattered. Thick shards of ceramic clattered to the floor. Blood ran down from the intruder's elbow he'd used to block the attack, but that was all the damage he'd sustained. It wasn't the knockout blow Nadine needed.

"*Found you!* Now, we have fun!" The words came out in a high-pitched squeal.

The masked man grabbed one of her wrists, and yanked Nadine out of the closet. She tried breaking free, but he was too strong. He held her in place as she screamed.

The masked man struck her over the head with the ax handle. Nadine's body slumped to the side in his grip.

"Quiet now?" he asked.

Nadine couldn't answer. The single blow had been all it took to knock her out.

"Good. Too much noise," the masked man said to no one but himself.

He threw Nadine over his shoulder and started out of the cabin.

The smell of hay and feces hit her nostrils before she even opened her eyes. Behind that, there was another pungent smell she couldn't place her finger on that made her nose itch. Nadine reached up to rub at her nose. The rattling of metal and cold steel digging into her skin made her eyes fly open.

She saw metal handcuffs around her wrists attached to chains, and wanted to scream, but couldn't. Her mouth was stuffed with a rag that tasted vile and used. There was thumping coming from somewhere behind her, reminding her of the banging back at the cabin.

The cabin. Right. That was the last place she'd been before waking up here…

Stephen.

Her husband had gone downstairs to make sure that everything was alright—and it hadn't been.

The thump came again. Faster, harder this time, easier to locate—and it wasn't coming from outside the barn. Or even from inside. It was her heart beating so loud it was in her ears.

Nadine sprang to her feet, and felt cuffs around her ankles, too. Enough moonlight came into the room that she could follow the chains. They fed down into the ground, then came back up and were attached to an old, gigantic machine. That meant she'd have to be able to move a ton if she was going to do more than crouch.

Her thoughts raced, settling finally on one question, *where am I?*

In front of her, what she had thought was a solid wall opened up around the frame of a door. Nadine squinted against the sudden light shining into her face, but kept her eyes open to see what was coming. The light revealed the bales of hay all over this place, they were stacked up almost to the ceiling. Their dry grass littered the floor. Bones and dark stains that could only be blood lay among the fallen pieces of hay, too.

In the doorway stood a silhouetted figure. Tall, broad-shouldered, with a significant gut that spilled out the sides as much as it did the front. He stood as if he was hunched over. She remembered him. The masked man from the cabin.

Her thoughts shuffled again. *I'm going to die.*

She screamed; the sound muffled by the rag in her mouth. But outside, in the dense woods that she had been so freaked out by on the way here, there would be no one to hear her.

The man moved forward, stepping into the light coming from outside the barn. He grabbed an electrical lantern from the wall and turned it on, then strolled toward her. Standing in front of her, he was even more imposing now.

Even worse, the glow of the lantern revealed him in terrifying detail. The mask on his face was ill-fitting, cracked, and peeling. The eyeholes were uneven, one much bigger than the other. The mouth part was cut out in a crude rectangle, like a child's first attempt at using scissors, but it was big enough that the man's thick lips protruded through.

He licked at them. The bottom of his tongue rasped against the leather mask as he did this.

No, not leather. Skin. Dear God...he was wearing someone's face...

"Hullo? Wakey, wakey!" he said in a voice that was much too loud.

Her stomach curled in on itself as she saw the dangling ears on either side of the face the maniac was wearing, saw the little hairs still stuck at the top of the dried flesh. She felt the tickle of vomit climbing up her throat. She fought against it, though, because she was sure to choke on it with the rag blocking its exit.

Fighting against it made her light-headed, and she thought she was going to faint. Nadine fought to stay awake. She had to stay awake. If he took the rag out, maybe she would be able to talk her way out of this.

"No, no," the masked man said, seeing her eyes starting to roll to the back of her head. "Awake. Awake. Stay awake. It better awake."

Nadine shook her head to comply—for her sake, not his.

The masked man bent down to be eyelevel with her. His lips were turned up into a grin that trembled like he didn't have much control of their facial muscles. He poked her on the temple with his index finger.

"You…stay awake. Fun is just beginning."

His voice…it was so childish, almost calming if it didn't belong to a three-hundred-pound man wearing a face over his head, and if she wasn't shackled inside of a remote barn deep in the woods and her husband…oh dear God, where was Stephen?

"I will take the rag out. You scream. If you want, you scream. Makes it easier."

He nodded to her, like a parent telling their child it's okay to fall over the first time the training wheels are taken off a bike. Then he pulled the rag out of her mouth.

The man rose up to his full six-foot-five height and walked over to a wooden shelf at the end of the barn. He opened a metal case that was sitting on the bottom level. It was heavy-duty, like something the military might keep their rifles stored in. But what the masked man pulled out wasn't a rifle, or even a weapon, really.

The moonlight glinted off the chainsaw as the man swung around. There was another happy, sloppy grin on his face as he trotted back to her.

Now Nadine screamed. She screamed until her throat hurt.

The masked man pulled the cord at the end of the chainsaw and watched in fascination as the blade begin to speed up and the little engine coughed and barked.

Nadine's screaming could be heard over the sound of it.

The masked man pulled the cord one more time, and the chainsaw revved to life.

"Fun for me!" he yelled out. "Not for you!"

"No! No! Please!" Nadine cried, watching the man inch the chainsaw toward her right leg.

"Yes! Yes!" he screamed back, but she didn't hear him, because Nadine went unconscious. She was out cold before the metal of the chainsaw bit into her leg, waking her again to a nightmare she couldn't escape.

ONE YEAR LATER

CHAPTER 1

Fred wasn't even settled in his room yet when his phone went off. He set his backpack on the computer desk and looked at the screen, the name GAVIN was displayed on it. Fred wasn't much in the mood to talk to him right now, but he'd been dodging his friend's phone calls all day, and if he didn't answer, Gavin would just keep calling until he did.

May as well get it over with, he thought, hitting the answer button.

"Hey man. Sorry, I was busy all day," he lied, slumping into the computer chair by his study desk.

"No worries," Gavin said from the other end of the line. "I know how it is. Finals are killing me."

"Yeah," Fred replied. *Now imagine if you had a job.*

He wasn't going to say that to him, but he sure thought it. Fred picked up a pencil and tapped its eraser against one of the spirals of a notebook on his desk. He was hoping Gavin would make this quick. He had studying to get to.

"But fuck school," Gavin cackled. "I'll be back in town this Friday."

"I know," Fred said. The words came out with more edge than he intended. He wanted to believe it was because of the long shift at the electronics store, but he wasn't sure that was the whole truth.

"Did you check out the link I sent you?"

"No, Gav, I haven't. Haven't had the chance." In fact, he didn't even know what link he was talking about.

"What the hell, dude!" Gavin said to him, then to someone else he yelled, "Fuck you too, buddy!"

"Are you driving?"

"Yeah, to my homie Beadie's house for a party. Can you say drunk freshman girls?"

Fred groaned. "Jesus man. Weren't you just complaining about finals?"

"Yeah, those are in the AM. Nights are for partying."

Fred laughed. It was kind of amazing that Gavin was an astrophysics major, on the Dean's list almost every semester, but yet somehow found time to party all the time.

"Nah, but seriously," Gavin continued. "I might see Brooke there. I'll tell her about the cabin."

"Cabin? What?"

"Holy shit, man. Did you not get my text messages or something?"

"I told you, I've been busy."

Gavin sighed dramatically into the phone. "I rented a cabin for the weekend. I sent you a link with all of the details—and you're coming. I'm not taking no for an answer."

"I don't know, man. I kind of just wanted to kick back and relax after the semester was over—"

"Shut up," Gavin said. "You're coming."

"I promised Noelle we'd hang out more when my time freed up."

"Are you an idiot?" Gavin said. Fred could practically imagine him facepalming. "Invite her! Chicks love camping."

Fred thought about that for a second. "Damnit, Gav. When you're right, you're right."

"Come on Fredster, it's our last summer before we turn into boring adults. Let's do it big."

If Gavin wasn't such a Brainiac, he would've been a hell of a used car salesman. This wasn't the first time that thought crossed Fred's mind because Gavin had a way of persuading people since they were kids. He was so effective at persuasion that people would come out convinced that what Gav wanted out of them was what *they* had wanted in the first place.

Fred was feeling like that right now and wondered why *he* hadn't come up with the idea. A relaxing summer getaway trip to a cabin in the woods. Was there a better setting to finally ask a girl to be your girlfriend?

"Fred, you still there?" Gavin's voice stirred him out of his daydream.

"Yeah, yeah. Yeah to everything."

Gavin laughed. "That didn't take much."

"Shut up."

"Look, even if Noelle says no, I'll make sure there're chicks. Don't worry about that."

"Do you ever think about anything else besides getting laid?"

Gavin ignored the comment and continued, "You think you can hit up Fletch? The weed up here is dirt compared to his stuff."

"Uh, yeah. Probably."

"Alright," Gavin said. "I'm at Beadie's house. I'll talk to you later."

"Okay, man. Later," Fred said, ending the call.

By later, Fred knew he meant he would drunk text him at four AM when he returned home from the party. It was kind of odd to Fred that he did this, but at the same time they were also each other's oldest friend.

They'd been friends since Gavin shit his pants on a field trip to the zoo in front of the whole class. Fred's mom happened to be chaperoning the trip and took him into the bathroom to clean him up and bought him new clothes from the zoo giftshop. After that embarrassing incident, none of the other kids wanted to sit and eat lunch with him, so Fred's mom made him share a table with Gav.

While drinking apple juice and eating their PB and J sandwiches, Gavin told Fred that he thought the smell of the animals would be strong enough to cover up the smell of his poop in his pants. They laughed so hard that juice came out of Fred's nose, and ever since then, they were friends. Best friends, even. But recently, they started to drift apart.

It was a combination of growing older and Gavin going to a school in upstate PA that started it. And now that Fred was busier with work to try to save money to get out of his parent's house before graduation, and Gav was still into the whole partying scene, their lives headed in complete opposite directions, drifting them further apart.

Fred grabbed his phone to check the link, feeling a little bad about ignoring Gav the last few weeks, but then thought better of it. He put the phone in his pocket, forcing it out of his sight so he wouldn't be tempted to open it up. He had studying to get to.

After a few minutes of staring at the pages in the microbiology textbook, the words started to run into each other, turning into continuous rectangular blobs of ink. Nothing his eyes passed over meant anything to him.

Frustrated, he slammed the textbook closed. Fred leaned back and stared up at the ceiling, fighting the urge to check his Instagram timeline.

Downstairs he could hear the murmur of his parents watching some cop drama—CSI or Law and Order, one or the other—which meant it was late, but not too late.

He thought about texting Noelle, but by the time she got back to him and he drove over to her neighborhood, it probably *would* be too late. He'd have to talk to her before the trip to invite her, obviously, but that would have to wait until at least tomorrow.

Thinking about the trip made Fred wonder what Fletcher was up to. He got up and stuck his head out one of the windows and looked down the street. The lights were still on at his house.

Nice. It was never too early to start stocking up for a camping trip. Plus, maybe a few hits would help him focus on studying when he came back.

Fred ducked back into the house, grabbed his keys off the desk, and headed out.

CHAPTER 2

"What's with the camera?" Andy Cameron said to the pair coming into his office. "She's not going to film with it, is she?"

"No, I'm not," Molly Sanger said. She could feel the death glare on her face, because even though the question was about her, he'd addressed it to her partner because he was the man of the group.

It wasn't surprising coming from a guy like Andy Cameron, who probably thought his expensive suits and flashy haircuts were enough to woo any woman he wanted. But just because it wasn't surprising didn't make Molly any less angry about it.

"Okay, good," Andy replied, reclining back in his chair. "I get nervous in front of the camera."

"Yes, yes, your concern is understandable. It could be quite a stressful ordeal to be filmed." Emeril Dantes, Molly's partner, settled into the chair in front of Andy's mahogany desk. Molly sat in the one next to him. "Molly and I have interviewed and filmed enough people to know not everyone is suited for it."

"You guys make films?" Andy said. He leaned forward in the chair. His eyes were wide with admiration. "What kind?"

"Documentaries," Molly answered.

"Very interesting," Andy said, but with any real interest fading away. He'd been hoping to hear they were in PA from Hollywood, or something along those lines. "Well, how can I help you? You guys have a place you want to rent out in mind?"

"Actually yes. We were interested in one of your cabins," Emeril said, reaching into his pocket and taking out a sheet of paper with a picture of a cabin printed on it. He placed it on the desk, right-side up to Andy.

Andy laced his fingers together and rested his elbows on the desk. It took him a few seconds to remember which of his many properties he was looking at, but then all the information flooded into his brain at once.

"Ah, yes. I see you've taken an interest in Lakewood Cabin."

"A great interest, actually," Emeril said, giving him a big smile.

"I assume you looked through the pictures on the website?"

"Mm-hmm." Emeril said.

"You've seen how beautiful this early twentieth century log cabin is, then?" Andy said, and for the first time glanced over at Molly.

She could only assume this was the part of his pitch when he tried to convince the wife or girlfriend of his usual clientele so that she would help him convince the man.

Poor sucker. He had no idea what was going on or who they were.

"Oh yes," Emeril said. "I did extensive research on the cabin, which is why we're interested."

Andy reached behind him where a number of brochures for hotels, cabins, bed and breakfasts, and beach houses were filed into a clear plastic shelf. He found the brochure for Lakewood Cabin, plucked it out of the slot, and splayed it out in front of them on top of the printed-out photo. The right flap of the brochure folded out into a miniature map of the area.

"See, if you look here, this path takes you to a nearby lake." Andy traced his finger over a trail that was aptly named LAKE WALK. The path went around a body of water named Willow

Lake that was represented by a blue blotch of ink on the map. "It's named after the willow trees that surround it—let me tell you, Mister Dantes, you'd be picking the best time of the year to stay at Lakewood Cabin. You have a kayak or a canoe?"

Emeril shook his head, not giving Andy the energy he was looking for. He was hoping the man would talk himself tired sooner rather than later. What he was doing was the verbal version of Mohammed Ali's rope-a-dope strategy, but something told Emeril that Andy Cameron had the aid of a certain white powder to keep him going and going longer.

"Do you plan on hiking? You look like you like to hike, Miss Sanger. Do you?"

"Sure," Molly said with little enthusiasm. She knew what was going on—it was the reason her and Emeril were partners. They could always follow the other person's moves without having to say anything to each other.

"Well, you're in luck, because these trails off the main cabin grounds are to die for!" Andy said, bringing his finger to another trail east of the cabin. This one was labeled HAWK'S VIEW TRAIL because it ended at a cliff.

There. There was Emeril's opening to take over. Turned out he didn't need the man to burn himself out after all.

"Funny you mention that," Emeril interjected.

Andy had his mouth open, ready to go onto the next part of his sales spiel but stopped. He looked up from the brochure at Emeril with an inquisitive look on his face. "I beg your pardon?"

"Funny you say the trails are to die for," Emeril repeated.

"Wh-what's that supposed to mean?" His eyes flickered over to Molly, then back to Emeril's, searching for the answer on their faces.

Emeril cleared his throat, and reached into the pocket of his shirt again, and took out another folded up sheet of paper. Like he did with the picture of Lakewood Cabin, he spread it out on the desk facing Andy. Andy immediately recognized the printout as a copy of a police report. It was of the Lang incident that happened last year.

"What's that? Where did you get that?" Andy said. His eyes were frantic.

Emeril leaned back in the chair. He interlaced his fingers and put his hands behind his head and smiled at Andy. "I told you, I've done extensive research into your cabin. I'm wondering if you've mentioned this incident to any of the previous renters?"

"What's it matter?" Andy said, shaking his head. "People can be murdered anywhere."

"Hmm, I see you dodged the question."

"No," Andy answered, hoping that would be the end of it and he could go back to trying to get them to rent the cabin. "What kind of an idiot would bring that up? It would scare people off."

"I see," Emeril said. He took out another piece of paper from his pocket and put it in front of Andy. "These are more reports of people who have gone missing in the woods. Many of the reports mention your cabin as a nearby landmark. I'm curious if you know anything about these?"

Andy looked down at the printed out reports like a teenager staring at pages of his not-so-secret-anymore diary. His face flushed red. "What's your point, Mister Dantes? Do you want to rent out the cabin or not?"

"I want to know what you know about these before I hand over any money—and why you think these people are going missing."

"I understand you're concerned about your safety," Andy stumbled on his words at seeing a smile flash across Emeril's face, "but I can assure you that Lakewood Cabin is a safe environment for you and your partner."

"I'm sure the Langs would disagree with that," Emeril said.

Andy was losing his cool and was starting to get frustrated enough to not care if he lost these two as clients. "Who are you two?"

"I am a paranormal investigator, Mister Cameron. My partner here is a documentarian. We investigate the odd, the mysterious, and the unexplained. These woods that your cabin is in, and the disappearances of these people, happens to fall into all three categories."

Andy grabbed a tumbler from a shelf under his desk, took it over to a miniature fridge and dumped some ice cubes into it. He came back into the chair, reached under the desk for his secret stash of whisky he sometimes drank when he worked late at nights at the office, and filled his cup to the rim.

"Okay, Mister Dantes, Miss Sanger. I'll be honest with you two."

"Thank you," Emeril said. "That would be appreciated."

"Funny stuff does happen in the woods around Lakewood Cabin. I have no control over that. And it's true, I don't tell potential renters about these missing persons reports. I suppose that's dishonest of me—maybe even slimy—but I'm in the business of renting out getaway homes for people, not busting crime. That's what law enforcement is for. Can I ensure your safety out there? No. Of course not. But, I can suggest having a good time and making sure your life insurance is up to date."

"Sure," Emeril said. "I have another question, Mister Cameron."

Andy took a big sip from his drink. "Go ahead."

"Why did the police write off the Lang incident as a murder-suicide? From what I've read, the wife's body was never found."

Andy shook his head. "I don't know. I suppose because the woods are too damn big to do a proper investigation. There's not really any one department assigned to the woods. The different townships pass around the responsibility like a hot potato. It all depends on who gets called when and all that."

"I see," Emeril said. "That's interesting."

"In case you haven't noticed, Mister Dantes, the towns around here aren't much of towns at all. Some of them have populations less than two thousand people. The sheriff and the milkman might be the same fucking person in some of these places for all I know."

"Hypothetically speaking," Emeril said, "if I wanted to find out more about these woods and the missing people, who would I consult if not the police?"

"Oh shit, I don't know. Maybe the locals." He rolled the question over in his head for a second, then a name popped into his head. "I know! There's a guy named Harold Buckley."

"Where can I find this Mister Buckley?"

"He's usually in the Green Lizard Tavern over in Prairie Town. I can give you directions there." Andy reached behind him, to the clear shelf where the brochures were again, and this time took a paper bar menu out of it. He handed it over to Emeril.

"I go drinking there sometimes. Harold Buckley is almost always there when I go. Weeknight or weekends. I think maybe he lives there. Maybe rents out a room in the back of the bar or something," Andy laughed.

Emeril glanced at the menu and then handed it over to Molly, who did the same before putting it in her purse.

"Fair warning," Andy went on, "he's a bit of a loon. Always talking crazy stuff, conspiracies and that kind of junk…er, I mean, is that what you guys do?"

"Something along those lines," Emeril said, ignoring the insult to his profession. This was something he'd learned to roll with early on in deciding to become a paranormal investigator.

"Now," Andy said, sitting up straight. He was feeling the whisky working its magic in him. "Can we get back to discussing Lakewood Cabin and how it's the perfect summer destination for you and this young lady here?"

"Actually," Emeril said, getting out of the chair, "we're not interested anymore."

"What!" Andy jumped out of his chair so fast the back of his thighs hit the chair. It rolled back on its wheels and slammed into the wall behind it. "B-but…but I told you all that stuff. Wait. You were never going to rent, were you? You tricked me!"

Emeril pulled out a hundred-dollar bill from his wallet and threw it down as he collected his printouts. "For your troubles. You did well on camera, Mister Cameron. Try not to be so hard on yourself."

Now Andy saw the red glowing light on the camera, one he should have seen before. Anger swelled up in him. "Hey, no! You-you don't have my consent to use that footage."

They'd started out of the office already, and Emeril was already outside. Molly turned to Andy Cameron, halfway out the door herself, and said, "We'll blur your face out, don't worry. No one will know it was you admitting to being slimy."

"Th-this isn't fair!" Andy called after them.

Molly responded by shutting the door behind her.

"It's amazing that people can be both stupid and rich," Emeril said as he slid into the Subaru's driver seat. He pulled his cellphone out, but he still had no service in this area. This far north in Pennsylvania seemed to be one big dead zone, with pockets of reception, instead of the other way around. Must be all the trees.

"I didn't know we had the funds to pay interviewees now," Molly said, getting into the passenger seat and closing the door.

Emeril snickered. "A hundred dollars for someone like Andy Cameron is nothing but pocket change. That was more an act of clearing my own conscience for the deception."

"Let me rephrase then: I didn't know we had the money to clear your conscience."

"We don't," Emeril said, putting the cellphone away. "But I think with the information he gave us we might be able to make a heck of a movie."

"Ah, so it was an investment?" Molly asked, but it wasn't exactly a question. More of a criticism than anything.

"Something like that." Emeril put the key into the ignition and started the Subaru up. They had almost an hour's drive to get back to their hotel.

CHAPTER 3

Fletcher Donovan was part Rastafarian-wannabe and part slick businessman. He was only two years older than Fred, but word was he owned the house he lived in, which was two houses down the street from where Fred lived with his parents.

He drove around in a two-year-old Lexus and was usually sporting the latest Apple Watch (which didn't fit in with his trademark image of blond dreads and a tie-dye shirt). Whenever anyone asked about his money, Fletcher told them he owned a car parts shop.

No one had ever seen or knew where this shop was located, but people didn't ask him too many questions because everyone in the town loved him. Not just the high school and college kids who he sold weed and shrooms to, but their parents loved him too.

Of course, they didn't know about the drugs, or if they did, they turned a blind eye. They loved him because of the help he did around the neighborhood. Fletcher and four of his buddies (who looked closer to his image than his flashy Apple watches) got together on Sunday mornings and went around picking up litter in the neighborhood. They did this about twice a month, and it was free of charge to the neighborhood—no one knew if Fletcher paid his friends or just gave them goods from his stashes, but again, this wasn't anyone's concern.

Fletcher and the same buddies also tended the communal garden they'd converted the front yard of the abandoned meat shop into. In the summer, residents could go and pick fresh cherry tomatoes, basil, carrots, cucumbers, and sometimes even catnip for their kitties. It all depended on what Fletcher and his merry band of modern-day hippies decided to grow that year, but either way, it was another bonus he had with the neighborhood adults.

Fred rang the doorbell, hoping his friend wouldn't think this was some sort of police drug bust since he'd forgotten to text him that he was coming.

An eye appeared at the peephole, then Fletcher opened the door with his usual big grin. His blond dreads were pulled back into a messy ponytail and he wore an oversized Dark Side of the Moon t-shirt.

"Freddie, my boy!" Fletcher hopped toward him and gave him a big hug. "Nice of you to stop by, man!"

Fred wasn't the biggest fan of being close to people, but because it was Fletch, he always let it slide. He reciprocated by patting him on the back, then pulled away. "Yeah, man, sorry. Been busy with school and work."

"I know how it goes," Fletcher said. He moved back into the house, leaving an inviting gap in the doorway. "You wanna come inside? I got some new records, come check 'em out."

The bit about the new records was both code for "come inside if you're looking to buy something illicit" and the truth, because Fletcher collected vinyl. Not in a hipster way, he'd been collecting those since they were in middle school.

Fred went inside the house and Fletcher led him into the living room.

The inside of the house always took Fred by surprise. It was clean and tidy instead of being dark and damp and smelling of BO and weed. It wasn't riddled with drug paraphernalia and roaches like one might expect a pothead's place to be. Fletch's place looked like it had been decorated by a hippie mom.

There was a large, red Indian rug underneath a bone marrow colored coffee table decorated with Buddhas. Various images of Vishnu, Ganesha, and psychedelic patterns hung in gold-plated frames on the walls of the rooms and corridors. The place smelled of a hint of weed, but the dominating scent was floral and smoky smells coming from the incense burning on the mantle over the fireplace.

Fred sat on one of the couches. It was large and soft, and the cushioning seemed to form itself around him. A stoner's dream seat.

Fletcher sat in a fan-backed wicker chair, picking up a cup off the center table filled with Coke and rum that had thick ice cubes floating in it.

"Want some?" Fletcher asked him, taking a sip of his drink.

"No thanks," Fred said. "Gotta get up kind of early tomorrow."

"Ah, well, what can I help you with then?"

"I need some of the good stuff," Fred told him.

"The good stuff, or the *really* good stuff?"

He considered this for a second. Gav would've said both if he were here, but the camping trip was a few days out, and Fred didn't want to stash a bunch of weed and shrooms in his bedroom until then. Not that his parents would snoop around when he wasn't home or anything like that, it just didn't sit well in his mind.

"Just weed," Fred said. Anyway, if Gavin insisted on it, he'd come pay Fletch another visit.

"How much do you need?"

"An ounce."

"Whoa! You having a party or something?"

"Sort of," Fred said. "A party in the woods."

Fletcher's eyes lit up. "A camping trip?"

"Yeah."

"Where at?"

Fred shrugged. He pulled out his cellphone and started searching through his messages from Gavin. "Not sure. Believe it or not, Gav planned this whole thing. We're going a day after he comes back from upstate."

"Rad, man." Fletcher took another sip of his drink and considered things.

While he was doing that, Fred found the name of the cabin they were going to. "We're going to this place called Lakewood Cabin. Ever heard of it?"

Fletcher shook his head. "Nope."

Fred opened up the website link and read a phrase off the banner webpage. "*The most secluded cabin in Pennsylvania.*"

"Talk about a good party spot, huh?" Fletcher laughed. "Hey, what do you say if I come? I'll bring the weed free of charge, just for letting me tag along."

"Wow, Fletch, that'd be awesome. The more the merrier and all that shit. Isn't it kind of sudden for you, though?"

"Nah. I can get some of my buddies to housekeep while I'm gone."

"Okay, then. Yeah, man, I think it'll be a good time." Fred didn't add that less than an hour ago he'd been arguing with Gavin about not going…

"Since you're here already, you want to smoke a little?" Fletcher jutted his chin out to a bong on the table between them. It had some sort of Chinese dragon on it, with gold characters all over it.

"Thought you'd never ask, Fletch," Fred said to him.

"You know I always got you, man," Fletcher said, switching the drink for the bong in his hands. Before getting it ready, he asked, "You sure you don't want a drink?"

"Nah, that's alright."

"Saving your partying for the camping trip?"

Fred laughed. "Not really. Just not in the mood."

Fletcher started the bong while they caught up. It'd been a while since they'd hung out, and Fred wasn't sure if it was the weed or what, but when he returned home later that night, he felt better about everything. The stressful day at the computer shop seemed so long ago that it wasn't weighing on him anymore. He even got some studying done and was looking forward to crushing finals week.

Before his brain went off for the night, he realized the pot had nothing to do with this new mood—and everything to do with the upcoming camping trip. A week away from suburban life surrounded by nature with plenty of food, drinks, and music by a campfire sounded like just the thing he needed after this semester of hell. And the cherry on top of it all would be that if things went the way he planned, Noelle would be there with him.

When he finally went to sleep, there was a smile on his face.

CHAPTER 4

Molly was sitting by the window, watching the light drizzle splash against the glass. Her laptop was open on the desk in the corner of the hotel room, with her headphones sitting next to it. She'd been editing the footage of the meeting with Andy Cameron for the last hour and a half or so, and now she was growing weary.

She looked down at the slender watch on her wrist and saw it was almost midnight. Her stomach grumbled, and in her mind, she saw Emeril putting down the hundred-dollar bill on Andy's desk. All she had for dinner tonight was a yogurt topped with some granola because she was trying to keep their costs down, and here Emeril was throwing money around like they were on the Coen Brothers's budget.

It was nights like these that made her regret choosing this profession. Her father, a hard ass military guy who'd become a criminal defense lawyer after getting out of the Marines, had wanted her to follow in his own footsteps.

Being a rebellious twenty-one year old at the time when she was applying for law schools, Molly never bothered to open their response letters. Instead, she'd decided to take all the money she saved while working at the local campus bar and travel around the country vlogging her experiences on YouTube.

She worked wacky jobs for money, slept in her car most nights, and lived off canned beans and jerky for about a year and a half. A year into it was when she met Emeril at a bar in Florida.

He approached her because he saw her talking into the camera at one of the tables and asked her what she was doing. At first, she thought it was just an old man hitting on her. Molly was no stranger to that—not that she was going to win any beauty pageants, but she was a thin blond at a bar by herself, which was usually enough for her to garner attention from drunken men.

But the more she talked to him, the more she realized he had no interest in her sexually. Even now that they were four years into making documentaries together, she wasn't sure Emeril was sexual at all. He never talked about past relationships or a marriage or anything like that. He was all about his research. It was kind of odd, like he was some sort of asexual alien or something, but she tried not to think about it too much.

That night they met, he told her he was a paranormal investigator. Molly started out thinking it was funny and played it up for the vlog audience, but Emeril didn't play along. He was adamant and stern about his beliefs in the supernatural, told her he was convinced that there was no way the five senses humans had could discover everything this planet had to offer. Emeril invited her to come with him to an abandoned house not far from the bar they were in.

Molly thought she was sniffing out some sort of trap to get in her pants, or maybe even worse—maybe this strange old man was planning to murder her. But Emeril didn't push it on her, just gave her his number and went back to drinking his scotch.

It wasn't until the next night that she called him back. For some reason, the encounter with him had stuck in her mind. The sincerity of his belief in the supernatural was like nothing she'd ever heard, but he didn't come off as some batshit crazy person. It was more like he had a staunch belief in this, more like a highly religious person who truly believed they were on a path God put them on.

Emeril had picked up on the first ring, and they'd arranged to meet at the same bar they met at the night before. From there, Emeril drove them to the abandoned, supposedly haunted Truman house. On the drive there, he told Molly all about the legend of the house.

The story went that a man had caught his wife in bed with another man. In an act of rage, he went down to the basement, grabbed his double-barrel shotgun and gunned down the pair while they were having sex in the master bedroom. Still blinded by rage, the man drowned his two children in the bathtub.

Supposedly, at specific hours of the night, you could hear the faint sound of the shotgun blast going off. In the bathroom, you were supposed to be able to hear the ghosts of the children splashing in the bathtub, struggling to get out from underneath their father's hold.

Molly found rational explanations for all of that during their visits. The sound of the ghost shotgun blast could have easily been the loose window pane banging against the side of the house when the wind blew. The splashing could be attributed to water leaking through the walls from the side of the roof, seeing how there were plenty of leaks in the ceiling.

Even though there seemed to be a rational explanation for the rumors, Molly was fascinated when Emeril walked her through the house. He was like some sort of tour guide showing her mind's eye the possibility of another world layered over top of their own.

She uploaded the vlog, and the next few days she saw her YouTube subscriptions almost double. The vlog of the paranormal investigation was a huge hit, and she called Emeril back and proposed the idea of them making a full-length documentary. She emailed him a breakdown of the ad revenue and how much she would be making on the vlog by herself. She told him that with his help, she could turn her channel into something bigger.

That was the hook, line, and sinker for Emeril, and the beginning of their documentary series. Emeril brought the knowledge, interviewing skills, and investigation, while Molly did all the camera work and editing. Together they were the Paranormal Talk channel on YouTube.

But what the cameras didn't show were the shrinking bank account numbers between revenue checks, the camera/computer repair bills, the shitty hotel rooms that smelled of cheap cigarettes, and nights of going to sleep hungry like she was tonight.

A knock on her hotel room stirred her out of her thoughts. She turned away from the water streaked window and went over to the door. Molly didn't bother asking who it was, because it could have only been one person.

She opened the door, and Emeril stood on the other side. The top of his chauffeur hat and the tips of the hair poking out from underneath it were wet from the rain. He held a brown paper bag that was dotted with water. A strong smell of cilantro and tortillas wafted from it.

"I brought you a burrito from the restaurant next door," he said, holding up the takeout bag. "A peace offering, if you will."

"For what?"

"For not consulting you about giving Andy Cameron money for the information."

"That's…alright, Emeril." She felt like a big jerk now that he'd gone out into the rain to get her food.

"Are you saying you don't want it?"

Molly grabbed the bag from his grip and shook her head. "No, no. I'm not saying that at all."

They went into the room. Molly pushed her laptop and headphones to a corner of the desk, and they ate their burritos on it.

"How was the interview? Did you get a proper angle?" Emeril asked.

"It's OK. It'll work." Molly took a big bite of her burrito, realizing she was hungrier than she thought. "My biggest concern is that he was hard to hear sometimes, so I'll have to pipe up the volume on some of his responses."

Emeril nodded in approval, then changed the subject. "On my way to get these burritos—if you can call these burritos—I had an interesting phone call."

"About what? And with who?"

"The bar owner over at the Green Lizard Tavern. About our friend Mister Harold Buckley."

"And?"

"And, he told me Mister Buckley wasn't in, but that I should try again tomorrow. He said there's a good chance he'll be there. Said the guy comes in every other night."

"How far is this place from here?"

"A little over forty minutes."

Molly finished off her burrito, crumpled the tinfoil wrap, and threw it in the wastebasket. "Guess we'll be putting a bunch of miles on the old Subaru out here, huh?"

Everything out here seemed to be spread out far apart, with either barren fields or dense trees between the places where people lived.

"Indeed," he said. "Hopefully she'll hold up."

Emeril finished his burrito and threw the foil into the trashcan with hers, then he got up. "Well, I'll leave you to edit or whatever it is you had planned for the rest of the night."

"It's almost midnight, Emeril," Molly said, flashing the face of her watch at him.

"Ah," Emeril said. "Well, it's almost ghoul and goblin o'clock."

They'd walked through the room, and Emeril was standing out in the hotel corridor. Molly was at the door. She rolled her eyes, and closing the door she said, "Good night, Emeril."

"Good night," he said to her before the door shut.

CHAPTER 5

There was a knock at Martin Barter's office door. He always hated disruptions when he was working on the schedule, especially in the summer when so many of the hotel maids needed days off.

But he painted on his best smile when Joey Schmitt, the kitchen manager, came into his office and slumped into the chair in front of him. The collar of his shirt had a ring of sweat around it, and his hair was all disheveled.

"Hey, Joey, what I can I do for you?" Martin said, closing the spreadsheet. Something told him this wasn't going to be a quick conversation.

"So this morning I get a fuckin' text from one of my cooks, tellin' me he quits!"

That was bad news, but not really Martin's concern. They could always find a replacement in this economy. "Okay…"

"Then I come into the kitchen, and guess what I see? Fuckin' grease all over the damn place. Like the little asshole—pardon my French, Marty, I'm just pissed—put it into a bucket and threw it all over."

"That's awful," Martin said, nodding. He already knew where this conversation was going.

"Think you can give me a hand, Marty?" Joey shook his head back and forth like there were gnats buzzing around his crown.

"Sure, I can send some of my staff to help you out." Marty said.

Joey nodded, then his train of thought went elsewhere. "I can't believe that little fuckin' weasel. That's the problem with young kids today—it's not like back in the old days when we were growing up. Back when you would get a foot up your ass for this sort of stuff, ya know?"

"Yeah," Martin said, despite that Martin was in his early thirties and Joey was at least in his mid-fifties. Sometimes it was easier to just agree with people.

Joey got out of the chair. "Anyway, enough of my bickerin'. You think something can be done before the breakfast rush?"

Martin glanced up at the clock on the wall. It was only six AM. The hotel kitchen wasn't officially open until 7:30 AM. He'd have to call in his big gun for this one. "Yeah, I have the perfect guy for it. I just gotta call him on the walkie."

"Okay, great," Joey said, getting out of the chair. "I'll meet you at the kitchen so you can check out the mess this prick left behind."

As Joey headed out of the office, Martin heard him muttering "can't believe it" and some more expletives.

Once he was sure the kitchen manager was out of the room and down the hallway, Martin burst out laughing. It was an unfortunate thing that happened to him, but Joey's way of handling stress always amused Martin. Usually his reaction to situations was overdramatic, with too many f-bombs, but once Martin would see the mess in the kitchen, he'd realize in this case his reaction was perfectly called for.

Martin took the walkie-talkie that connected with the rest of the cleaning staff's walkies. He hit the button on the side. "Hey, Ignacio, are you in yet?"

"*Yes, boss.*" The voice crackled through the speaker.

"Great. Can you meet me in my office? I have some extra work for you this morning."

"*Yes, boss*," was the response.

As it always was.

"See this shit? Unbelievable, huh Martin?" Joey said, a hand on his hip.

The two managers were standing between the fridges and the grill that made up the cooking area of the hotel kitchen. Towering behind them was the hotel janitor, Ignacio Calderon. A gargantuan man who was as wide as the two managers put together.

Joey hadn't been exaggerating, as he sometimes was known to do. The young cook had left behind a big "fuck you" before quitting. Grease was splashed all over the area. It was on the counters, the floor, the crevices between the appliances, and so on. It was about two gallons of the stuff, and the worst part was that it had turned into a sticky, thick goo after cooling overnight.

"Yeah, I'm seeing it alright," Martin sympathized.

"Think your guy can do it? In an hour or so?" Joey said, checking the watch on his wrist as if making sure that time hadn't suddenly jumped ahead.

Martin turned to Ignacio. "What do you think, big guy? Think you can do it in an hour?"

Ignacio didn't respond, because his mind was elsewhere…

The brown spots of grease were changing color before his eyes. First, a bright red. The color of roses, maybe, but the spots got darker the longer he stared at them.

Darker. Darker. Darker.

Until they were crimson. The same shade of red as drying blood.

Ignacio was no longer in the hotel kitchen. He was in Mexico now. In the house he grew up in until he was a teenager. His father was teaching him how to cook huevos con chorizo. Even though Ignacio was only six years old, he was already tall enough to tower over the stove.

Arturo Calderon was standing behind him, his hand over Ignacio's hand holding the spoon they were using to scramble the eggs.

"Just like this, Mijo," Arturo said, guiding his hand around the rim of the pan, then bringing it straight down through the puddle of runny eggs. "Keep doing that over and over until it starts to get fluffy. Entiendes?"

Ignacio nodded.

Arturo let his hand go and watched his son unsteadily make circles around the pan with the spoon. Ignacio kept looking over at him for approval.

"Bien, bien," Arturo said, leaning against the countertop with his arms folded. "It's important you know how to cook eggs, Ignacio. They'll help you get stronger. You want to get stronger, don't you?"

Ignacio could still feel his chin burning and pulsing from the punches the kid who beat him up after school had landed on him. They were going to turn into bruises tomorrow. He nodded to answer his father's question.

Arturo clapped him on the shoulder, and was about to say something else, when Guicho Calderon—Arturo's younger brother—came charging into the room. He was dragging an older teenage boy by the arm. The kid's eyes were opened wide and wet with tears.

"I finally caught the pendejo," Guicho said, forcing the kid into one of the metal chairs at the kitchen table.

Ignacio knew who the kid was from seeing him around the village. His name was Cristian Morales, nicknamed "Canguro" because when he got into fistfights at school, he danced around like a kangaroo.

Ignacio didn't know this, because he was too young to know the extent of his father's business, but Canguro was one of Arturo's low-level drug dealers. Mostly he sold ecstasy to young adults outside of nightclubs and bars in downtown Veracruz, nothing too serious. But still, Arturo wasn't nicknamed "El Toro Macho"—the Alpha Bull—for no reason. Whenever someone owed him money, as Canguro did, he made sure to make an example of him.

"Sir, sir. I have some of your money—I got robbed—" Canguro started, but Guicho slapped him on the back of the head to get him to shut up.

"What're we going to do with him?" Guicho asked Arturo.

"Same thing we always do. Put his head on the table." Arturo wasn't leaning against the countertop anymore; he was standing straight and reaching into his back pocket for the knife he always carried there.

Ignacio watched his father's face transform from the one he knew, his fatherly face so to speak, to the one he wore when handling business. It was almost like a dark shadow was cast over his father's face, and his eyes were about ready to shoot flames out of them.

He looked over at Canguro, who must've noticed the same thing Ignacio did, because he was bawling now. In between sobs, Ignacio pieced enough words together to figure out Canguro was begging to not be killed.

And the look on his father's face, as scary as it was, was nothing compared to the face when Ignacio made a mistake and was about to get a whooping. Ignacio thought Canguro would've shit himself if he saw that *face.*

Guicho did as he was told, and slammed Canguro's head on the table. Canguro tried to turn his head, but he was too slow, and his lip busted on impact. Guicho held his head down, while the kid screamed and bled on the table.

"Hey, Arturo, you think we should tell him to leave?" Guicho said, referring to Ignacio.

Arturo looked over at him, almost as if he'd forgotten his son was there. He shook his head. "He's old enough by now."

"He's six," Guicho reminded him, and then immediately regretted challenging his brother when Arturo shot him an icy glare.

"Shut up and worry about doing what I tell you," Arturo barked.

Guicho didn't respond. He was too afraid to.

Arturo took his knife out of the sheath, laid the sheath down on the counter behind him, and then went over to Canguro. "How much do you have on you?"

"I—I have two-hundred pesos, señor." Canguro answered through bloodied, quivering lips.

"How much does he owe, then?" Arturo asked Guicho.

"Three-fifty."

"Listen here, escuincle." Arturo grabbed Canguro by the top of his ear and pulled hard on it. The kid yelped. "If we catch you tomorrow and you don't have my money, I'm going to do more than pull on your ear, you understand?"

"Y-yes, yes. I'll have it, I promise—"

"Shut up. Don't talk unless I tell you to," Arturo said with an edge to his voice.

Canguro nodded as much as he could underneath Guicho's pressure. He stopped crying at the thought of being let go harm-free. But he wasn't going to be. No one that owed El Toro Macho had ever been let go harm-free. That was how he got that nickname and reputation in the first place.

With his free hand, Arturo reached down and grabbed Canguro's wrist, and slammed his hand on the table.

"No, no, no, please!" Canguro cried.

"What did I say?" Arturo yelled. "Speak without permission again and it'll go worse for you."

Canguro started to sob again but fought the urge to plead for mercy.

Arturo moved the pressure from his wrist to the middle of his hand, forcing Canguro to splay his fingers out. Then, he took the knife and started sawing his pinky finger off.

Canguro screamed like Ignacio had never heard anyone scream. Each slice forward and backward on the finger changed the pitch of his yell. It was like each motion was a different note, like his father was playing some sort of horrifying instrument.

There was a pop as the knife sawed through the bone.

It excited Ignacio. Excited him a lot.

The knife finally went all the way through Canguro's finger. Blood oozed out from both the detached finger and the wound on his hand, pooling on the surface of the table.

"You get the message?" Arturo asked, grabbing him by the hair. Guicho had stepped back to give him room.

Canguro nodded. "Y-yes! I'm sorry—"

Arturo threw him against the countertop, the one Ignacio was standing by, and he jumped back out of reflex. Canguro's ribs hit against the edge, and he bounced off it dramatically and turned around to face what was coming next. At the same time, both his hands reached behind him to brace himself against the countertop.

Ignacio watched his wounded hand smear blood onto the white countertop with the fascination of a child watching an artist painting. Only this was touching a part of him he didn't know existed until now… He didn't have the word in his vocabulary then (or even now), but it was the morbidly curious part of him that was excited by the sight of the red blood.

He looked over at the cut finger, still sitting on the kitchen table, and felt the same thing. He wanted to touch it, but when he looked at his father, he saw he was still wearing his business face.

Arturo was pinning Canguro against the counter, holding the blade up to his throat. "What did I say about not talking? Do you think I'm fucking around, pendejo?"

Canguro shook his head and closed his eyes tightly, squeezing fresh tears out of them.

"Good. Now, remember. You get my money, or I'll cut your ear off next," Arturo said. "You think the ladies are going to want some payaso with one ear?"

Canguro shook his head again.

"You have permission to speak now. What are you going to have tomorrow?" Arturo asked him.

The kid opened his eyes to look into Arturo's face, to see if the permission to speak wasn't some sort of trap. Then he saw Arturo getting irritated with his stalling, and blurted out, "Your money, señor... I'll have your money."

"Good," Arturo said, letting go of the front of his shirt. Then to Guicho, he said, "Get him out of my face."

Guicho went over and hooked his arms under both of Canguro's armpits the same way he'd dragged him in here, but this time Canguro was going willingly. He was crying silently, which also was different.

Ignacio watched Canguro's bleeding hand continue to drip blood as he left the room with Uncle Guicho. The floor was checkered black and white, and the blood turned a dark purple when it stained the black. And yet, on the white, it was bright red. This was the first time Ignacio realized how beautiful blood was.

"Ignacio, the eggs," Arturo said.

Ignacio snapped out of his trance and turned to the stove. The eggs were burning at the bottom, and smoke was rising out of the pan. Ignacio reached out for the spoon and did the twisting motion his father had just taught him.

He looked over at Arturo to see if he was doing it right, and his father's face had lightened up. He was back to being his dad teaching him how to cook breakfast, not the mean man who takes care of business.

Ignacio was as fascinated with his father's ability to change faces as he was with the sight of the blood. He hoped to grow up to be like him one day and be able to wear many faces.

"Hey, Ignacio, you okay?"

Martin stepped closer to him and saw the man's eyes were glazed over as if he was on some downer drug trip. If Ignacio wasn't so gargantuan, he would've snapped his fingers in front of him to try get him back to earth, but no way was he going to risk pissing off a guy this big. He didn't think even him and Joey together could take this lug.

Thankfully, Ignacio snapped himself out of whatever was going on. He shook his head, and said, "Sorry, boss. Tired."

"Yeah, I get it. It's early," Martin said, unconvinced.

Joey, who had been growing impatient at the janitor's immobilization because they were pressed for time before the breakfast rush, repeated the question they were waiting for him to answer, "Well, big guy, think you can handle this?"

"Yes," Ignacio finally answered.

"Great!" Joey said. "Come on, I'll show ya where the slop sink is at in the back."

CHAPTER 6

Fred and Noelle were at Twisted Treats, sitting on a bench and trying to get as much enjoyment from their ice cream cones as they could before the summer heat turned them into melted messes all over their hands and napkins.

Fred was nervous to ask Noelle to come camping with him, and this wasn't even *the* big question. But dammit, she looked cuter than ever in her Legend of Zelda stained-glass pattern dress. She'd also done something with her hair, lightened it or something that made it almost look silver.

If she said no, that meant Fred would be out in the woods doing dumb stuff with Gav while Noelle was hanging out at the dive bars down in the city where all the guys that were slim and tall and dressed better than Fred hung out. One of them would surely catch her attention—or the other way around, whatever—and make moves on her. There's no way that wouldn't happen to a girl like Noelle.

Fred swallowed some of his rocky road ice cream while he worked up his courage. If he never asked, he'd never know what her answer would be. He cleared his throat and said, "Hey, Noelle, I know this is kind of sudden, but you wanna go camping this weekend?"

"Hm?" she said, swallowing the lick of strawberry ice cream in her mouth.

"Gav—you remember him?"

She smiled. "How could anyone forget him?"

Yeah, of course. Now that he thought about it, the first time Noelle met Gavin he was hammered at some party. He was being a particularly big asshole that night by throwing limes at some people in the middle of a game of beer pong.

"Well, he planned some camping trip for the weekend. I know it's such short notice and all—"

"Let me check my schedule," with her free hand she reached into her dress pocket, but when the hand came out it was empty.

Fred's eyebrows knitted in confusion.

Noelle laughed and put her hand on his shoulder, "It's summer, silly. Of course I'm free. Your friend going to be okay with me tagging along?"

"Gav? Oh yeah. He'll be more than okay with it."

Noelle gave him a sideways glance but didn't press him on what he meant.

He wasn't about to tell her they already talked about her, and that it'd actually been Gavin's idea to invite her. No reason for her to know about that at all.

"This weekend, right?"

"Yeah. At some place called Lakewood Cabin. Supposedly the most secluded cabin in PA."

"Ooh, how exciting," Noelle giggled.

Fred joined her by laughing, then they talked a little bit more about the trip. The conversation lost its steam after a few minutes, and they sat back on the bench to finish their ice creams in silence, watching the birds fly in the summer sky, feeling the golden sun touching their shoulders.

They were glad that it was summer. Glad to be alive. Glad to be young.

And thought it would be like this forever.

CHAPTER 7

The 1997 Toyota Camry went through a narrow passage between two large oaks and entered a clearing of trees. Pinecones and nuts littering the ground crunched underneath the tires as the car came to a rolling stop.

Ignacio got out of the car. The car's suspension system squeaked in relief of his three-hundred pounds. He looked between the trees and saw that the sun was only halfway below the horizon. It was later than usual because of the kitchen clean-up job his boss needed him to do this morning, but there was still at least an hour or two of sunlight left.

Ignacio grabbed his gym bag from the backseat, slung it over his shoulder, and hurried home.

Ignacio's home was a farmhouse in an abandoned campsite. The farmhouse had once belonged to the family that owned the camp, but those days were long gone. The place was Ignacio's now. And as far as he knew, no one knew this campsite existed.

Which was good. He meant to keep it that way, too. That was why he parked the car far away, in case someone heard his car driving through the woods and followed him, he wouldn't lead them back to his home.

It would be bad if someone found where he lived. They might ask questions. Ignacio didn't like being asked questions.

In his bedroom, Ignacio changed into his hunting outfit, which was a camo vest and dark brown leather pants he made himself. The combination of these two colors made it so that if he was standing, he would blend in with the trees. If he was crouching, he would look like one of the bushes. Ignacio was tall and wide enough that both effects worked.

He grabbed the sheathed machete hanging on one of the walls and slung it by the strap to his back. Then he went to the shoddy dresser next to his bed, and from the bottom drawer took out a butterfly knife. He slipped it into his back pocket, blade first so that the handle peeked out into the air, just like his father used to carry his knife. He was no "Toro Macho," but this was the moment in preparing to go hunting when he most felt like him.

But there was still one more piece to his hunting outfit—quite possibly the most important part of the whole thing.

Ignacio went to the small closet, the one that always had its door closed until this moment, and threw it open. Inside the closet sat a rack of homemade masks hanging from hooks like at a Halloween store. Only these weren't made of rubber, and they weren't representations of peoples' favorite trademarked characters, either.

These were leather masks made from the faces of his human victims. Ignacio had constructed them on a sewing machine himself. He'd learned how to sew by watching his mother make his *luchador* masks every Halloween. That was all Ignacio wanted to ever dress as. One year it might've been El Hijo del Santo, another year Blue Demon, and yet another Mil Mascaras, but it was always a luchador.

In his childhood room, he used to hang these homemade luchador masks the way the leather masks hung in his closet now. He would put them on when no one was home and leap off the furniture performing various moves he saw luchadores performing on the television.

The highest point Ignacio had ever dared to jump off was the television set. He could still remember flying through the air, elbow drop aimed at the pillow he put on the ground, imagining himself leaping off the wrestling ring turnbuckle at a flattened out opponent.

While he was going through the air, he'd come up with the name of his alternate persona: Varias Caras—Many Faces. It was a name that was fit for a luchador, but eventually became the name of the monster that lived inside of Ignacio.

He grabbed one of the masks and slipped it on over his head. It was the face of Stephen Lang.

The transformation was complete. He was ready to go hunting.

Varias Caras was awake.

It didn't take him long to find prey.

Varias Caras watched the campers from behind a thicket of bushes. The man was bent over a pit, trying to get a fire going, but the only thing that was burning was his temper from the frustration of not being able to start it.

The woman he was with was by a picnic table, seasoning up some cuts of meat. Pork chops, maybe. Whatever it was, it made Ignacio's stomach grumble.

Ignacio watched them a little longer. There was only one tent set up in the area, which meant it was likely just these two, but it was always important to make sure. That way, no one could sneak up on *him* while he was distracted.

The couple continued to go on about their business. The man was cursing and throwing his arms aggressively through the air now. The woman kept looking over her shoulder, trying to soothe the man's temper with words of encouragement.

Each time she turned her head, her eyes passed over the bushes Ignacio was hiding behind, but she was too oblivious to see him.

The prey never noticed him until it was too late.

Out here, campers felt safe. Ignacio wasn't sure why, especially since there were scary animals, but people always had their defenses down when they were out in the woods.

It didn't occur to Ignacio that his heightened sense of hearing allowed him to realize all the danger lurking around in the wilderness better than anyone. His hearing was so sensitive he could hear the heartbeats of large predators—such as bears and bobcats—miles away.

The better part of that was that he could hear the heartbeats of prey, too.

And right now, the young couple's heartbeats were at a steady, normal pace, but they would be thumping in his eardrums soon enough. Ignacio took the machete out of the sheath on his back and prepared himself for the loud sounds that came with killing.

"We should've just gone to fucking Puerto Rico, instead," Chad yelled out to Paige as he threw the piece of flint and stick into the firepit. "This shit ain't working."

"I'll just YouTube a video and we'll figure it out," Paige said, wishing she could be more help. She was grateful her sister lent them the portable charcoal grill to cook up the pork chops. At least they'd be able to light that if they couldn't figure out how to get a fire going.

"There's no service out here, how the hell are you gonna pull up a video?"

"Oh. I hadn't thought of that."

Under his breath Chad said, "Do you ever think of anything?"

In that moment, he hated her. But really, it had nothing to do with her. He was just angry that he couldn't get the fire going.

Chad stood up from the crouch, and started for the cooler next to their tent. As he was going across the campground, out the corner of his eye, he saw the bushes move. He looked over in that direction, and saw a gargantuan man pop out from behind them. The object in the man's hand—his mind was so scrambled he couldn't discern what it was—glinted in the light.

As he emerged out of the hiding spot, Ignacio took a backseat and let the monster take over.

Varias Caras swung the machete through the air as he charged at Chad. Despite the danger, Chad was frozen in a state of disbelief. Varias Caras hacked his head clean off his shoulders with a single swipe. The head sprinkled blood all over the dirt as it soared over the campsite. Chad's decapitated body fell backward.

Varias Caras shifted his focus over to the woman, who'd had enough time to figure out what was going on and started running. It did little good for her, though, as she blindly ran into the picnic table in front of her. Paige tripped on one bench, flipped over the tabletop, and banged her head on the bench on the other side before hitting the ground.

She tried to pick herself up, but her limbs were jelly and she fell back to the ground. She started to crawl through the dirt, trying anything to get away, but it was futile. Varias Caras caught up to her and dropped a knee down into her back.

"PLEASE, NO! NO! DON'T KILL ME!" She tried to squirm from underneath him, but there was no give, it was like someone had just dropped a piano on her.

Varias Caras grabbed her head with both hands, and in a quick motion broke her neck. Her head was turned all the way around, so that the girl would have been looking up at him if she weren't dead.

He looked at her face for a second. She was pretty, but she wouldn't make a good mask. Her face was too small, and the skin was too soft. Even as leather, it would rip if he tried to squeeze his head into her face.

She'd be good for food, though.

He got off her and looked around again, making sure one last time that it was indeed just those two here. After a quick three-sixty sweep of the area, he was reassured. He picked up the girl and put her on his shoulder.

Later, he would return for the guy's body and dismantle their entire camp setup. Tent, coolers, bags, all that. Their SUV he would drive deeper into the woods where no one would find it or to a nearby body of water where he would put it in neutral and then roll the vehicle into it, effectively erasing any traces of Chad Richardson and Paige Silver ever having been out here camping in these woods.

Of course, their families would eventually file missing person reports with the local police, but what good would that do?

By then, Ignacio would have already started to eat them.

CHAPTER 8

THE BARN DOOR opened, and the afternoon light came pouring in, waking Nadine. She sat up, blinking against the sudden brightness straining her eyes.

Her eyes adjusted after a second or two, and she was able to make out the blobs of colors coming toward her as her captor. He was pushing a wheelbarrow, with two bodies piled on it. They were both naked, well-toned, young-looking (mid-twenties, if she had to guess), and covered in blood.

This didn't shock or scare her anymore. After a few dozen times of watching her captor bring dead bodies into the barn, she'd become desensitized to seeing murder victims. When that'd happened, when dead bodies no longer repulsed her, no longer made her stomach queasy, she'd accepted this barn as her new reality. She was sure of two things: she'd never see the outside world again except for when her captor opened the barn door, and she would die here.

Varias Caras stopped with the wheelbarrow in front of her. Nadine saw one body was headless. The one stacked on top of it wasn't, but the head was twisted around facing the wrong way.

"Good morning, *mi hermosa*." He said to her. *Good morning, my lovely.* That was one of the ways he greeted her. Sometimes he called her beautiful, sometimes precious.

There was a sick satisfaction to hearing those terms of endearments. They made her feel good despite that they were coming from a person she hated, but he was the only human contact she'd had in… however long it was since she'd first woken up here. Hearing those words, and still being able to understand them, were the only things that kept her from losing her grip on the last shreds of her humanity she was holding onto.

Varias Caras bent down and planted a kiss on her forehead. His lips felt like warm, raw sausages against her skin. She shivered, and thought about pulling away anytime he did this, but she was afraid of how he'd react. She didn't really have the energy to do it, anyway.

"I have food," he said, looking at the dead bodies with a satisfied smile. Then he glanced over at the trough of beans and frowned at seeing it was almost empty. "I bring food for you later, okay?"

Nadine nodded.

"Have work to do first." Varias Caras told her, tilting the wheelbarrow forward slightly. He started for another room in the barn, one that was located behind the wall Nadine was chained to.

It was the room she'd come to think of as the Butcher Room, because it was where he took the bodies of his victims to cut into pieces. He would emerge from that room with Ziplocs stuffed with cleaned, trimmed, raw meat. If she didn't know any better, she would have assumed it was pieces of chicken or pork or maybe some wild bird. But she did know better, and she didn't need to ever see inside the room to know that that was where he turned the humans he killed into the cuts of meat he cooked.

Nadine had no choice but to listen to the sound of a butcher knife slamming against a wooden surface in the other room. Occasionally, clumps of meat would hit the ground with wet thuds. Bones would crack as they were pulled apart from

CHAPTER 8

The barn door opened, and the afternoon light came pouring in, waking Nadine. She sat up, blinking against the sudden brightness straining her eyes.

Her eyes adjusted after a second or two, and she was able to make out the blobs of colors coming toward her as her captor. He was pushing a wheelbarrow, with two bodies piled on it. They were both naked, well-toned, young-looking (mid-twenties, if she had to guess), and covered in blood.

This didn't shock or scare her anymore. After a few dozen times of watching her captor bring dead bodies into the barn, she'd become desensitized to seeing murder victims. When that'd happened, when dead bodies no longer repulsed her, no longer made her stomach queasy, she'd accepted this barn as her new reality. She was sure of two things: she'd never see the outside world again except for when her captor opened the barn door, and she would die here.

Varias Caras stopped with the wheelbarrow in front of her. Nadine saw one body was headless. The one stacked on top of it wasn't, but the head was twisted around facing the wrong way.

"Good morning, *mi hermosa*." He said to her. *Good morning, my lovely.* That was one of the ways he greeted her. Sometimes he called her beautiful, sometimes precious.

There was a sick satisfaction to hearing those terms of endearments. They made her feel good despite that they were coming from a person she hated, but he was the only human contact she'd had in… however long it was since she'd first woken up here. Hearing those words, and still being able to understand them, were the only things that kept her from losing her grip on the last shreds of her humanity she was holding onto.

Varias Caras bent down and planted a kiss on her forehead. His lips felt like warm, raw sausages against her skin. She shivered, and thought about pulling away anytime he did this, but she was afraid of how he'd react. She didn't really have the energy to do it, anyway.

"I have food," he said, looking at the dead bodies with a satisfied smile. Then he glanced over at the trough of beans and frowned at seeing it was almost empty. "I bring food for you later, okay?"

Nadine nodded.

"Have work to do first." Varias Caras told her, tilting the wheelbarrow forward slightly. He started for another room in the barn, one that was located behind the wall Nadine was chained to.

It was the room she'd come to think of as the Butcher Room, because it was where he took the bodies of his victims to cut into pieces. He would emerge from that room with Ziplocs stuffed with cleaned, trimmed, raw meat. If she didn't know any better, she would have assumed it was pieces of chicken or pork or maybe some wild bird. But she did know better, and she didn't need to ever see inside the room to know that that was where he turned the humans he killed into the cuts of meat he cooked.

Nadine had no choice but to listen to the sound of a butcher knife slamming against a wooden surface in the other room. Occasionally, clumps of meat would hit the ground with wet thuds. Bones would crack as they were pulled apart from each other. A trash bag would rustle as unwanted parts of the bodies were thrown in it. Meanwhile, Nadine reluctantly pictured what was happening in the Butcher Room, and she wanted to cry, but there was no spirit left in her broken soul to do so.

CHAPTER 9

The Green Lizard was a pretty standard small-town bar. Most of the place was taken up by a wooden bar with stools in front of it. Small tables with silver napkin holders and condiment containers on them were crammed against the walls, and more stools sat on either side of them. There was a colorful jukebox that lit up purple, blue, red, yellow, and orange all night long that didn't see any action until later at night, when the patrons were drunk (or close to drunk) and they wanted to sing along with "Sweet Home Alabama" or sway to Journey's "Don't Stop Believing."

Luckily, it was too early in the night for the scene to turn into that and there were only three patrons in the bar when Molly and Emeril came in. The most raucous person in there was a short man in plumber's coveralls. A big, shiny wrench hung from the side of his utility belt in comical fashion, and he was throwing his hands through the air as he complained to the bar tender about his work day. Opposite the plumber was a burly old man who was staring through the glass of dark beer in front of him. He looked like he wouldn't bat an eyelid if you waved your hand between his gaze and his drink.

The man Molly and Emeril were looking for was at a corner table, sitting underneath a row of framed Beatles records hanging on the wall. The two of them must have stuck out as outsiders, because Harold Buckley immediately waved to them. Molly couldn't help but notice the fingerless gloves the man was wearing.

"Hey there folks," the lanky bartender greeted them. He seemed to be relieved at the temporary distraction from the plumber's ear beating. "Can I grab ya something to drink?"

Emeril shook his head. "No, thank you. We're here to meet somebody."

"Sure," the bartender said. "Go on right ahead. If ya need anything, I'm here all night."

"Thank you," Molly said.

They both went over to the table where Harold Buckley was sitting with a cold beer and a plate of cheese fries in front of him. Besides the leather gloves, Harold wore a wrinkled shirt with a faded Dr. Pepper logo on it. His shaggy hair was a disheveled mess on his head, and he reeked of marijuana.

"Hey, you the ones who were looking for me last night?" Harold asked, smiling at them.

Apparently, the bartender had told Harold about the phone call Emeril made last night.

"Yes," Emeril said, sticking his hand out to him. "My name is Emeril Dantes."

Harold shook his hand. "Harold Buckley."

Molly and Harold shook hands and introduced themselves. Then Emeril and Molly sat on the stools across from him.

"What can I do for you?" Harold said, picking up a cheese fry and munching on it.

"We're paranormal investigators doing research in the area," Emeril said, cutting to the chase. "We'd like to ask you some questions."

"Whoa." Harold dropped the half bitten french fry on his plate and sat up. He looked over at Molly, then back to Emeril. This was like a dream come true for a conspiracy theorist like him. "Seriously?"

"Yes," Emeril said. "Seriously."

"That's… rad." Harold shook his head to re-center himself, then said, "Well, what're you researching exactly?"

"The disappearances that happen in the woods around here." Emeril left it vague on purpose, to see what he would volunteer.

"Ah," Harold said, grinning from ear to ear. It was rare that he ever had these kinds of conversations outside of the internet forums he frequented. Most people in real life lost interest in these sorts of topics quickly. Either that, or feigned interest out of courtesy—which was just as much of a bummer. "You want to know about Camp Slaughter?"

"Camp what?" Emeril wasn't pretending here. He didn't know what he was talking about.

"Camp Slaughter," Harold repeated.

"Hold on," it was Molly who interjected. "Harold, do you mind if I record this?"

"Like video?"

"Yeah," Molly said. "For a film we're doing on our investigation."

"Someone pinch me," Harold laughed.

"What?" Emeril said again.

Harold laughed harder. "Nothing. Just, wow. I can't believe I'm going to be in a film about Camp Slaughter."

Molly took that statement as his agreement to being recorded and took her cell phone out. It was easier to do these types of interviews from her phone rather than with her camera, even if the quality wasn't as good, because the camera attracted too much attention in public places like bars. Using the camera would mean she'd have to edit out all the distractions of curious passersby asking what they were doing or if they were making a movie to turn the recording into a seamless interview. The phone was more discrete and less interesting to those not involved. It was OK, though, because sometimes the spliced in low-res scenes added to the atmosphere of the documentary.

Molly pulled the plastic stand on the back of her phone case and pointed the camera at Harold.

"You recording already?" he asked, running a hand through his messy hair.

"Yeah," she said, moving the phone to get him more centered into the frame. "Okay, go ahead. You guys can continue."

"Mm-hmm," Emeril said. "Let's back up a little for the sake of the camera and introduce yourself."

Harold's grin somehow grew. "My name is Harold Buckley. I'm thirty-four years old. Um, I work at a mechanic repair shop. I have no kids. I own a dog—a mutt, some sort of bulldog mix, I think. I'm really into conspiracies and scrimshaw—"

"Okay, Mister Buckley. That's quite fascinating, but more than enough for an introduction," Emeril said, giving him a fake smile.

Harold fidgeted in his seat and let out a nervous chuckle. "Okay, okay. Sorry. That was a joke, by the way—the scrimshaw bit, I don't actually do that."

"Right," Emeril said. "Try to act natural, Mister Buckley. Pretend the camera isn't even there. We can cut out any flubs or stumbles, so there's no pressure."

"Sorry," he apologized again, then fixed the glasses on his face. "Not every day you get to be in a movie, you know?"

"We know," Molly said.

"You were telling us about a Camp something-or-other before we started filming," Emeril reminded him.

"Ah, yes, yes." And bringing the topic back to conspiracies seemed to be the key to Harold relaxing. "You said you were investigating the people who go missing in the woods, right?"

"Yes."

"The word is that those people have all found a place in the woods called Camp Slaughter. It's supposedly a campsite that's haunted by malevolent spirits, and anyone who gets near it is killed by the ghosts."

"Have you ever seen this so-called Camp Slaughter yourself?"

Harold shook his head. "Heck no. The woods give me the heebie-jeebies. I've just done extensive research on the place from behind my keyboard. Safer that way, right?"

"So, is this Camp Slaughter place real?"

"Who knows? No one's gotten pictures of it, or if they have, they didn't live to share them." Harold ran one gloved hand through his hair again. "But it doesn't matter."

"Why's that?"

"Because I don't think it's ghosts or anything goofy like that out there."

In Emeril's mind, Harold Buckley had just graduated from whack job to a potential legitimate source. "What do you mean by that, Mister Buckley?"

"Oh, ho, ho, are your pants on tight, chums?"

"Uh, sure," Emeril said, questioning his own judgment for the moment.

"I think the ghost stuff is a load of bunk. I think what actually happens is that there's some cannibal out there—maybe even a whole family—that kills these people in the woods for food."

"What leads you to think that?" Emeril asked.

"Remember how I said there's no pictures of Camp Slaughter?"

"Yes," Emeril said, a tad annoyed considering the man had just said that a few seconds ago.

"That's not quite entirely true." Harold reached into the pocket of his dingey chino pants and pulled out his massive cell phone. He tapped a few buttons on the screen, then held it out to them.

The picture on the phone made their stomachs lurch and glad they hadn't eaten dinner yet. They were looking at a blurry picture of a necklace made of human ears dangling up high on a tree.

"Holy shit," Molly said. "Are those human ears?"

"*Ding, ding, ding!*" Harold said, pointing at her. "Someone posted this picture anonymously online. No one has any idea who the source is."

"How can you be sure that this is even in the woods around here?" Emeril asked, folding his arms across his chest.

"I guess you never can be, but this picture was uploaded in an album with pictures from woods that are clearly the ones around here. There were multiple pictures of Willow Lake and the cliff where Hawk's View Trail ends."

Those were two landmarks that Andy Cameron had also brought up when he thought Emeril and Molly were trying to rent out his cabin for a summer vacation. This strange character seemed to be more and more promising by the second.

"Pretty freaky, huh?" Harold said, putting the phone down.

"What's this have to do with the Camp Slaughter place?"

"Oh!" Harold smacked himself on the forehead. The leather from the gloves muffled the sound some. "I almost forgot."

He pinched his fingers over the phone screen to zoom in on the picture, then turned the phone over to them. "See those blurry, squarish things in the back? People online debate for hours whether those pixels are cabins or not. Of course, the ones who think they're cabins also think that's Camp Slaughter back there."

Emeril nodded. "Fascinating."

"Indeed, it is," Harold said.

"A campsite with stories of ghosts and evidence of cannibalism happening near it." Emeril said this more to himself, but the next question was very much directed at Harold Buckley. "Tell me, which do you think is more likely?"

Harold stuck the phone back in his pocket and grinned from ear to ear again. "Come on, Mister Dantes, you're the paranormal investigator. *You* know which one I would bet on to be true."

"For the camera," Molly said to him. "Can you say which one you think is more likely for the camera?"

"Sure," Harold said, and looked right into the iPhone's camera lens when he said, "Methinks there's some human eating human out there."

Emeril didn't respond, but he agreed with Harold Buckley—and something told him Molly did, too. But she didn't say anything, either.

This interview turned out to be more informative than they thought it would've been, and there was a lot for them to process.

A lot to chew on, if you will.

CHAPTER 10

"Whatever, I don't give a flying fuck!" Wayne Briggs screamed into his Xbox headset.

The friends he was playing Fortnite with laughed at his outburst, so he took the headphones off and slammed them on the floor. "You guys are a bunch of virgin pussies anyway!"

In the game sphere, it didn't matter that Wayne himself was a virgin, too. An insult was an insult.

Today was an off day. Usually he was pretty good at the game, but he found himself at the receiving end of multiple kill streaks for the last hour or so, and his friends had been letting him know that he sucked relentlessly.

Whatever. Wayne was getting bored of the game, anyway, considering he'd been playing it nonstop since school let out. The only breaks he'd taken were to eat, hit the bathroom, watch some Twitch, or to masturbate.

As a result, his room smelled like farts, used socks, and whatever microwavable meals he was gorging on that day. It was only a matter of time until the scent would travel out into the corridor and his parents or Gavin would yell at him to clean his room. Until then, *fuck cleaning*, he thought. It was summer.

Now that he had the headset off, he could hear his brother talking on the phone down the hallway in his own room. Wayne couldn't make out the words exactly, but the tone of what he was saying was upbeat. He tiptoed (though he wasn't sure why) across the room, and slowly opened the door. He stuck his head out in the hallway to better hear what his brother was saying.

"Yeah, bro. Tomorrow at nine AM." There was pause as Gavin waited for a reply from the other end. "It's about an eight hour drive."

More pause.

"Yeah, that's why it's billed as the 'most secluded cabin in Pennsylvania,' numb-nuts." Gavin laughed.

Wayne wasn't sure who he was talking to, but from the sounds of it he had some sort of trip planned for tomorrow. An idea popped into his head, and he ducked his head back into his room and ran to his bed where his cellphone was.

It was eleven at night here, which meant it was nine in Cabo where his parents were on vacation. They'd still be up. Even old people stayed up past nine when they were on vacation.

Wayne dialed his mom, and prepared his best "good boy" voice.

"Brooke is bringing her friend Vanessa—she's some Instagram model or something—*and* her cousin." Gavin raised his eyebrows, even though there wasn't anyone around to see it. A lot of his antics, although others might have a hard time believing, were for his own amusement.

Gavin had taken his phone call down to the kitchen, where he was currently going through the freezer for something that would make a good late-night snack. He settled on one of the frozen pizzas, took it out of the box, and popped it into the oven.

"Like I told you, Fredster, I got the chicks covered," he said, settling into one of the chairs and kicking his legs up on the kitchen table.

"That's cool and all, but Noelle is coming," Fred told him.

"Wait, what, she is?"

"Yeah, I didn't tell you?"

"No. I mean, it doesn't make a difference, but I bugged Brooke to bring friends. I wouldn't have been such a—"

"Such an annoying prick about it?"

Gavin laughed. "You took the words right outta my mouth."

"Seriously, though," Fred said, "the more the merrier, right?"

"Bigger party. I like how you think." Gavin smiled.

Fred was thinking more along the lines of, the more people there were, the more everyone would be distracted, and he and Noelle would have more one-on-one time. He didn't tell Gavin that, instead he just said, "Yeah, that's the whole point of this trip, isn't it?"

"Oh yeah," Gavin agreed.

"Okay, man. I'm gonna let you go. I'm tired."

Gavin looked at the time on the front of the oven. It was pretty late, but he had to wait for that pizza to finish cooking and then eat it all before going to sleep. "Okay, yeah. See ya tomorrow."

Fred got off the phone with Gavin after making sure for the fourth time this week that the plans hadn't changed. They'd meet up at his place at eight-thirty to be on the road by nine in the morning, just as they'd agreed before, but with Gavin one could never be too sure.

Fred opened up his laptop and plugged it into the printer on his desk. He put himself in charge of the printout directions to the cabin because he trusted himself with the task more than he trusted Gav. He'd said he had them already, but again, one could never be too sure with him.

After going into Google Maps and printing out multi-page packets of directions, Fred decided to do a little more research into this place. He hadn't looked at anything since the night he opened the link to show Fletcher, because as it turned out he'd picked up extra hours at the computer shop. The only day he'd had off he spent with Noelle and helping his father with yardwork and fixing up the back deck to get it ready for summer barbecues. There'd been no time for him to look into this Lakewood Cabin place until now.

It was the night before their trip, but whatever. Better than not looking into it at all.

He glanced at the first five results on Google. It was generic information on the cabin, trails around the area, maps to print out, activity suggestions, and so on. Fred scrolled down and hit the next page. The headline of the first article at the top caught his attention:

COUPLE NEVER RETURNS FROM 'MOST SECLUDED CABIN IN PA'

Fred scanned the preview of the article to make sure it was about the same cabin. It was.

"Holy shit…" Fred whisper-screamed because it was late at night and his parents were asleep in the next room. Before he could click the article open, his phone buzzed.

Noelle was calling.

Fred closed the laptop and picked the phone up. "Hey, what's up?"

He crossed his fingers, hoping she wasn't canceling on him.

"Hey, not much," she said. "Sorry I called so late. I just can't sleep."

"That's okay. Me neither," Fred said, and chortled into the phone. He felt his face flare red with embarrassment. For some reason, he always found talking to girls on the phone more nerve-wracking than in real life.

"You guys still picking me up at eight?" she asked.

Fletcher had volunteered to drive his Jeep up to the cabin, and he was going to pick Fred and Noelle up before they swung over to meet with the rest of the group at Gav's place. It didn't make too much sense, considering they'd have to drive past the turnpike exit to get to Gavin's neighborhood, but Gavin insisted on this and no one wanted to argue with him.

"Yeah," Fred said. "I actually just got off the phone with Gav about it. We're sticking to the plan, as of right now."

Noelle laughed. "What does that mean?"

"Oh, I won't be surprised if Gav doesn't wake up before nine." Fred let out a short chuckle, grateful that this one came out much more naturally than the last.

"Well, if anything changes, let me know. I'll probably be up all night."

"You have insomnia or something?"

He'd meant it as a joke, but Noelle's response came out flat—suggesting it wasn't her going along with the joke. "Hm, something like that, I guess."

"Oh, shit. That...that sucks. Sorry."

"It's alright." She laughed to try to lighten the mood.

"You excited about the camping trip?" Fred asked her, hoping a change of topic would erase his stupid blunder of a joke.

"Yeah. I haven't been camping in a good while. Not since I went with my sister two years ago."

Fred knew all about Noelle's younger sister, and how she'd died in a car accident two winters ago. It was an accident that involved both of them that only Noelle survived. That was all he knew, but it was info enough to darken the mood of the phone call.

He swallowed, more nervous to talk to a girl on the phone than ever. "Well, hopefully you have fun on the trip."

"I hope so too." After a few seconds of silence, she added, "I'm sure I will."

"I'll try to make it fun for you."

"Thanks," she said, and then yawned.

"You should try to get some sleep," he suggested.

"That's probably a good idea," she said. "See you tomorrow?"

"Bright and early," Fred said, giving her an exaggerated groan. He was glad the conversation was out of delicate territory.

"Alright. Good night," she said.

"Good night, Noelle."

The call ended, and Fred immediately realized how exhausted he was. He locked his phone screen and shoved the laptop into the corner of his desk, then went to the bathroom to prepare to go to sleep. When he was done with that, he collapsed into bed and fell right asleep.

The article of the missing couple at Lakewood Cabin wouldn't cross his mind again, not until he saw just how secluded the woods they were going into were.

CHAPTER 11

Noelle laid in the bed, wide awake. The last time she'd looked at the clock it was two AM. It'd been two hours since she spoke to Fred on the phone, and she hadn't gotten even a wink of sleep.

The anxiety—it wasn't insomnia as Fred Meyers had suggested—wouldn't let her mind rest. She couldn't stop thinking about Rachel. Noelle hadn't meant to bring her up and make the conversation with Fred awkward, but her damn anxiety sometimes took over her mind. The tidbit about the last time she'd gone camping being with her little sister had flown out of her mouth before she realized she was saying it.

And once it'd been out there, there was no taking it back.

Noelle turned to her side. It was a more comfortable position, but she still wasn't going to be able to fall asleep.

Not until the anxiety ceased…but before that would happen, the hallucinations would have to begin and end.

They started fifteen minutes later.

Rachel was leaning by the window, the one with the blinds always open because Noelle enjoyed seeing the sunlight cutting through the room first thing in the morning. Rachel's skin glowed, and Noelle wasn't sure if it was from the streetlamp outside the house or a part of the hallucination.

Noelle was very much aware that it wasn't her little sister in the room, and it wasn't a ghost either. This was her mind tricking her into seeing a physical manifestation of the guilt she still held onto in the form of her sixteen-year-old sister—at least, that's what the psychologist told her.

Just because she was aware of that, it didn't make seeing Rachel *feel* any less real.

"About time you come to see me, again," Noelle whispered, aware that if her parents heard her speaking to her hallucinations in the middle of the night, they would start to worry even more about her mental state.

Rachel looked away from the window, and Noelle almost jumped off the bed. The skin on the right side of her face was hanging off, revealing all the veins and tendons underneath it. The hallucinations always came with injuries—sometimes the ones her sister actually sustained during the accident, sometimes fictionalized. But by now, Noelle couldn't remember which were which anymore.

"What? Do I have something on my face?" Rachel said. The part of her face that was intact smiled.

Noelle shook her head. "No, Rach. You look fine. You look beautiful."

Rachel grabbed the edges of her beige dress and did a small curtsy. "Thanks. Remember this dress? It was yours."

Tears filled Noelle's eyes, but she was smiling. She nodded.

Of course she remembered. She'd let her sister wear the dress on her first day of high school after years of Rachel begging her to let her wear it to the mall. She was convinced that it would complement her skin well—and she'd been right. Even back then, Rachel was always the more fashionable of the two.

Rachel crossed the room and lied down on the bed next to Noelle, her good side up. She swiped a thin finger under Noelle's eye to clear the tear away. "Don't you have to be up early tomorrow?"

"I do. But, you're here, and I miss you. I miss you every day, Rach."

"I miss you too, but you'll be miserable in the morning if you don't get some sleep. Like that one time before school when we were fighting for the bathroom and you chucked a hairbrush at my face." Rachel laughed. It was soft and almost-wheezy, just as it'd been in real life. The hallucinations got even that right.

"Didn't you get a black eye from that?"

"Yep. You big jerk." She laughed again.

"I don't think I ever apologized for that." Noelle's eyes dropped down to the mattress.

"That's okay." Rachel put her hand on Noelle's shoulder and guided her to lay down flat. "You don't have to."

"There's so much…" Noelle was flat on her side again. "Rachel, there's so much I should've said to you before… before the accident."

"Don't worry about it, Noelle. Everything's fine." Rachel touched her cheek. Her hand was soft and small. "Just sleep, okay, sister? Sleep, and everything will be A-Okay."

"You promise?" Noelle asked, feeling like *she* was the younger sister.

Rachel nodded. "I promise."

Noelle closed her eyes and said, "I love you, Rachel."

She couldn't hallucinate that her sister said it back to her, because a second later she was fast asleep.

CHAPTER 12

"Did you sleep on it?" Molly said, sitting down in a chair in front of Emeril.

They were in the hotel café, sitting by the window. A few of the people walking by on the sidewalk glanced a little too long at them as they tried to figure out what their relationship was. Some thought they were a father and daughter duo, while others probably thought Emeril was a rich old man who scored a much younger woman. Both were wrong of course, because they were nothing more than business partners.

Emeril closed his laptop and put it to the side. "I stayed up researching these Camp Slaughter rumors."

"And?" Molly said, making a mental note of him not answering her question and to ask it again if he didn't come around to it.

"There are others besides Mister Buckley who think the cannibal story might be true," Emeril said.

"Okay, well, what're you thinking, Emeril?"

He tapped his fingers on the table. The vibrations caused the black coffee in the mug in front of him to ripple. "I think we've got an even more interesting film on our hands than we thought."

Molly leaned back in the chair, realizing for the first time what she'd been hoping his answer would've been. They'd started out venturing to this small Pennsylvania town thinking they were making a documentary about haunted woods, but after their meeting with Harold Buckley, even Molly, who was the skeptic in the pair, was thinking this was all too coincidental.

Something strange was indeed going on in the woods around here, evidenced by the pages of research Emeril had shown her when first proposing the idea for the movie. And if she had to gamble on the truth of the matter, she and Harold Buckley would be betting on the same horse.

The thought that they were going into some sort of cannibalistic deathtrap made her uneasy. It almost made her want to tell him they didn't get paid enough for this shit (which was true) and walk away from the project, but she couldn't do that to Emeril. They were business partners, and on some level even friends.

"You're thinking something." Emeril said, picking up on her discomfort.

"It's just—well, the cannibal stuff. The ears, and all that. What if we're just jumping onto a cannibal's dinnerplate?"

Emeril smiled. "You have a way with words."

"Seriously, Emeril."

"I'm serious, too. You have a funny way with words."

"Are you going to address what I said, or keep dodging?"

"Every movie we've done before took us somewhere dangerous. If Bigfoot didn't get us in the Pacific Northwest, there were plenty of known predators that could've gotten us."

"That's different."

"Why's that?" Emeril challenged.

"Because the chances of Bigfoot 'getting us'—to borrow your phrase—are nil. And the wild animals are a threat people have been dealing with for years."

"You're saying there's a higher chance that the cannibal stuff is real than not."

"I'm saying that cannibals have existed in human history, but humans haven't been in contact with enough to know the proper way to fend them off."

Emeril took in a deep breath. At the same time, he took his chauffeur hat off and wiped his brow with it. "Sometimes I forget you're not a believer."

That statement, coming from anyone else, would've made Molly laugh. "I'm just saying, Emeril, the danger seems more plausible out there than anywhere else we've investigated."

"I understand," Emeril said.

There was a pause between them. Emeril picked his coffee mug up and took a sip to fill in the silence.

"So," he said, swallowing the coffee. "You don't want to do the movie?"

"I'll do it," Molly said. "I'm just airing out my concerns to you."

"Sure. Feel free to anytime," he said, nodding.

Molly felt like there was something he wanted to say but hadn't yet. Or maybe wouldn't say was the right way of putting it. Either way, she felt like there was a gap in the conversation that hadn't been closed.

Emeril opened the laptop and made a circle over the trackpad with his finger to wake it. "Besides the research, I've been communicating with our pal Harold Buckley."

He turned the laptop to face Molly. Gmail was opened on the screen with a chain of emails between the two of them. The last message that Harold sent to Emeril was the one that caught her eye:

From: TheLivingTribunal87@hotmail.com
I've got some possible locations of where the camp is. Let me know if you're interested. $150

"The idea is, if those pictures of the ear necklace are real, then the location of the campsite would lead us to the cannibal's hideout."

"Right," Molly said. "But that's quite a steep price he's asking for. Especially if his maps lead us to nowhere."

"Indeed," Emeril said. "We'll take it out of my royalties."

Molly saw the gleam in Emeril's eyes. The man wanted to find this cannibal hideout. All of the movies they'd made before turned out to be debunking the myths of the area, but this one he felt was a winner. Because somewhere deep down inside, maybe in the deepest recesses of his heart, Emeril didn't believe in this paranormal stuff.

But this one… This one had a possibility. This was the Moby Dick he'd been chasing. If they could uncover some cannibal's lair out there in the woods, all the time he'd spent chasing ghosts and aliens would be vindicated in one moment. This meant more to him than the $150 (or $250, counting what he'd paid Andy Cameron), which in the grand scheme of things wouldn't mean anything if they found the cannibal hideout.

"Alright, Emeril," Molly said, fidgeting in her seat. "Get the maps from him. Let's find out what's really out there."

CHAPTER 13

GAVIN WAS WAITING for them at the front of the house when Fletcher pulled the Jeep up to the curb of the cul-de-sac. He had an expression like someone had just thrown sweaty socks at his face.

"What's wrong with you?" Fred asked through the open passenger window.

"Got bad news," Gavin said, shaking his head.

There was a collective sense of worry from the three kids in the vehicle, thinking it had something to do with the cabin rental and their trip was off.

"What?" Fred finally asked.

Gavin leaned against the car and crossed his arms. "I gotta bring my little brother with me. He called my mom last night. My parents are down in Mexico and he gave them some sob story about how he's going to get lonely all by himself in the house so now they're making me take him."

Another collective feeling went through the Jeep, this one of relief that it wasn't anything serious. Fred looked over at Fletcher and rolled his eyes.

"So, what? What's the big deal?" Fletcher said, grinning.

"He's annoying," Gavin spat.

"What else? You get a hangnail or something?" Fred said.

Fletcher and Noelle laughed, and even Gavin's scowl disappeared from his face. He got off the car and glanced at Noelle in the backseat. "Uh, no. It's that Brooke's cousin is a guy. Dalton. His name is Dalton, like from *Roadhouse*."

"Oh God," Fred said, throwing his hands up in frustration. "Gav, are you guys ready to leave or what?"

Gavin ignored his question and barreled through with the point he was trying to make. "Glad you're here Noelle, otherwise we'd be taking too many sausages to this party."

"Well, nice to see you, too, Gavin," Noelle said.

"Let's stop wasting time," Fred complained. "We have a long drive."

"Alright, alright," Gavin said. "But hey, Fletch, can you do me a favor?"

"Yeah, what's up?"

"Can you take Wayne with you?"

Fletcher shrugged. "Sure."

"Sweet. Thanks. I don't need his ass in the same car as me for the next eight hours."

Funnily enough, Fred was thinking the same thing about Gavin. At least Gavin's little brother, who was only fourteen, had an excuse for his immaturity.

"Any of you want to come inside? Hit the bathroom or anything?"

They shook their heads no.

"We're good," Fletcher told him.

"Alright, well, we're all packed up and loaded, so I just gotta round everyone up. Then we're off to the cabin." Gavin slapped the side of the Jeep and started for the house. Halfway up the driveway he turned around, threw his arms up in the air, and yelled, "Get excited, fuckers!"

Fred hoped the eight-hour drive would sap him of some of his energy…but knew that probably wouldn't be the case.

Four hours later, they were stopped at a gas station built on a hill that overlooked the vast wilderness surrounding them. They'd left behind the suburbs three hours ago for farmland and left the farmland behind for woods an hour after that. Every now and then, they would drive by a small town or a remote house, but even those were being left behind the closer they got to Lakewood Cabin.

Fred stared out at the seemingly endless wilderness. Every cliff, valley, and hill he could see was covered with trees that had little to no separation between them. It was all so dense that if someone was down there and waving for help, he wasn't sure he would be able to see them.

The gas pump clicked, announcing that it was done filling up the Jeep's tank, but he still couldn't take his eyes off the beautiful landscape.

Gavin clapped him on the shoulder, startling him and making him spin around.

"Fletch put you on gas-attendant duty?" Gavin asked.

"I guess so," Fred laughed. "He's inside getting extra snacks."

Gavin looked over at where the girls were taking pictures for Vanessa's Instagram, using some of the scenery that Fred had been appreciating a moment ago for the background, and said, "Man, Noelle's looking fine as wine with that hair. No wonder you're so into her."

"Ugh, dude, come on. Don't fuck this up for me by being all…weird and aggressive," Fred pleaded.

"I won't, I won't. I'll be chill, man." Gavin clapped him on the shoulder again. "For real, though, Fredster, I'm glad you came. It wouldn't have been the same without you."

Fred caught the slurring at the end of his last sentence. "Gav—have you been drinking?"

Gavin put an index finger up to his lips. "*Shhh*. They don't know. They think it's just Pepsi in my cup."

"Jesus, dude."

"What?" Gavin stood straight. "I'm not drunk or anything. Just feelin' good. It's not like there're any cars on the road all the way out here."

"I don't care, it's still dangerous. And *we're* on the road with you, dummy."

"Okay, okay, fine. I'll ask Brooke to take the wheel. Alright?"

Fred scanned his face to see if he was telling the truth or not. He knew him well enough to know when he wasn't. Usually a flicker in his eyes gave him away, but this time he wasn't lying.

Before they could say anything more, Wayne yelled out from the pump in front of them that the Honda was done being filled up.

"Put the pump back in its place and put the receipt on the car seat," Gavin called to him. "Then go into the store and get me a Gatorade."

"A-are you serious?" Wayne asked, crossing his arms.

"Yeah, shithead. Now hurry, I'm thirsty."

"Fine," Wayne said, then started putting the pump back in its place.

As punishment for making their mom bring him, Wayne had to do everything Gavin told him to do or else he wouldn't let him drink on the trip. Wayne wasn't entirely sure if his brother would hold up his end of the bargain, but for now he was playing along. He'd be pissed if his brother snubbed him, but if he didn't, the payoff would be huge. He'd get to brag to his friends (both on Xbox and in school) that he got to drink beer and hang out with hot college girls in the woods over the summer. Shit, if he got lucky enough, he might even get to see a pair of boobs.

That was the only reason Wayne decided not to make a bigger fuss and headed into the store.

"Idiot forgot the receipt," Gavin said, watching the receipt flap in the wind. Then to Fred he said, "Don't be mad at me for drinking and driving. You know I'm always screwing things up."

"It's alright," Fred said. "It's cool, man. Don't get all sentimental on me."

Gav let out a chortle before starting back to his car. "I'll kick your ass if you tell anyone I got like this—there's something in the air out here that's got me acting funny."

They laughed at this, then Gavin was at the other pump, taking his receipt and complaining about how much it'd cost to fill up the tank.

Fred turned his attention back to the valleys and mountains in the distance. Gavin was right, there sure was something different in the air out here. Something that told him they were part of a small number of people who'd ever ventured this far into the wilderness.

Noelle and the two other girls were returning from their impromptu photoshoot, so Fred brushed these thoughts away, straightened up, and tried to act normal. But it was hard to do, especially since the headline about the missing couple popped into his head: *Couple never returns from 'most secluded cabin in PA'*.

CHAPTER 14

"Eight...six...five...eight..." Ignacio had to say the combination out loud, it was the only way he would put it into the lock correctly.

His brain didn't work like other peoples'. It never had.

He opened the locker and stripped out of his coveralls. They smelled, so he set them on the bench behind him and grabbed his gym bag from the locker. Ignacio took his regular clothes out from the bag. Today, his regular clothes were a beige shirt and his homemade leather pants. They were the same ones he'd worn when he hunted the young couple in the woods the other day. Ignacio slipped them on.

As he was putting on his shirt, there was a knock on the door. Martin Barter, the man whose name Ignacio couldn't remember but knew as "the Boss," opened the door and came into the room carrying an envelope in his hand.

"Hey there, Ignacio. How was work?" Martin asked.

Ignacio didn't say anything, just nodded to let the Boss know it was good.

"Great," Martin said, then extended the envelope out to him. "You weren't going to leave without taking this, were you?"

Ignacio grabbed the envelope. "Yes. I forgot."

"That's okay," the Boss smiled, showing white teeth underneath a blond mustache. "Glad I caught you before you left. Joey said to thank you again for the help."

"Joey…?" Ignacio thought he'd asked the question under his breath to himself but realized he hadn't when the Boss answered it.

"Yeah, the cafeteria manager. Remember? You cleaned the kitchen for him the other day?"

"Yes," Ignacio said.

"He was quite impressed. Said you left that place spotless."

Ignacio nodded. "Yes."

"Well, Ignacio, I better get going." Martin started heading for the door. "Taking the family up the mountains this weekend. You have any plans?"

Ignacio nodded. "Party. Party for my mamá."

"Oh," Martin said, taken by surprise because up until now he had no idea the man had family. Actually, he didn't really know *anything* about the guy except that he was a hard worker. "That sounds exciting. Lots of people coming?"

More thinking. Then he said, "Yes. Lots of people. Mamá likes people."

"Wonderful. Hope you have a fun time." Martin started out the door. "And remember, payday is every fifteenth and the last day of the month."

"Yes, Boss," Ignacio said, but he knew he wouldn't remember. It was hard for him to remember stuff.

Just as that thought crossed his mind, he *did* remember something.

"Boss!" Ignacio called out.

Martin stopped with his hand on the doorknob. "Yes, Ignacio?"

"Ignacio has present for you," he said, smiling proudly.

He opened the side pocket of his gym bag where there were two sandwich bags packed with dried-out meat sticks. One bunch was darker than the other, and Ignacio couldn't remember which one was his and which was for the Boss.

Uh-oh. Ignacio thought. *Should've marked them, tonto.*

He wracked his brain, trying to figure out which one was meant for the Boss, but couldn't. His brain had done him good up to this point, and now it was back to not working right. Worried that the Boss would be angry at him for taking too long, he committed to grabbing a bag and handed it over to him.

Martin took the sandwich bag. It was packed, almost to the point that the bag could burst it was so full. "Beef jerky?"

Ignacio shook his head, grinning. "Deer. Homemade. It's good for you, Mamá says."

Martin took a whiff of it. "Smells spicy."

"Oh yes," Ignacio nodded. "Dried peppers."

"This'll be a great snack for the mountain trip. The kids love jerky. Thank you, Ignacio."

"Yes, Boss."

Martin headed out the door.

A few minutes later, Ignacio had all his stuff packed and headed out of the building. The whole time hoping he'd given the Boss the right bag. If not, he'd just given him the last of his special meat sticks.

He would be bummed out if he did.

Deer meat tasted good. But human meat was better.

CHAPTER 15

Emeril was in his hotel room, looking over the maps he'd just paid Harold Buckley for. They were scans of existing maps with handwriting on them. For a brief second when he'd opened the files and saw what they were, his old heart fluttered at thinking he'd been duped.

But the more he inspected the maps, the more convincing they came to be. The drawn-on paths weren't just random scribbles as he first assumed. They seemed to be deliberately drawn, and when he compared them to the existing printed paths, he saw the geometry was similar.

His laptop binged, alerting him that a new e-mail came in. It was from Harold.

> **From: TheLivingTribunal87@hotmail.com**
> **I think the most promising one is file 3.**
> **How do they look to you, PI?**

Emeril closed the browser tab with Gmail open. He wouldn't have an answer for his question until they investigated the sites.

And, at the same time, depending on the dangers the maps may lead them to, that might mean he would never answer Harold's question.

CHAPTER 16

"WHOA," FRED HALF said, half gasped as the Jeep pulled into Lakewood Cabin's driveway behind the Honda.

Everyone climbed out of the vehicles and met in front of them. They all stared at the solid, two-story wooden cabin in amazement. Being that they were suburban and/or city folks, they'd never seen anything quite like this.

But it wasn't just the sight of the place, either. It was the smell. The air was crisper, fresher, filled the lungs easier. Out here there weren't many cars to pollute, and plenty of trees breathing oxygen into the atmosphere. They could almost feel the cleanliness on their skin.

"This is beautiful," Brooke said.

"For once, Gav, you weren't blowing smoke up everyone's ass." Fred said.

The group had a small laugh at this, then they fell back into awed silence, listening to the songbirds in the treetops and the buzzing crickets in the bushes.

"It's nice alright," Gavin said, breaking the silence. "So are you guys planning on just staring at the cabin or are we going to start unpacking sometime soon?"

Despite his disruption of the serene moment, he was right, and the group started to move. Except for Dalton and Vanessa, who were posing for selfies in front of the cabin, everyone went to the back of the vehicles to unpack their bags.

Gavin scowled at those two, and then headed up the driveway toward the cabin.

"Where are you going?" Brooke said, seeing him climbing the porch steps.

"Inside," Gavin told her without turning around. "I'm not unpacking shit. Wayne's pulling my weight."

"What the hell, Gav!" Brooke said.

"Eh, I wouldn't bother," Fred said to her. "He won't change his mind."

Brooke nodded. To Wayne she said, "Bring his shit in last."

Wayne looked over to see where his brother was and saw him at the front door fidgeting in his shorts pocket for the keys. Sure that his brother wouldn't see, he gave Brooke a big smile and a thumbs-up as his response because he was too tongue-tied that a college girl was talking to him to speak.

"Attaboy," Brooke said, rustling his hair, and then heading over to the back of the Honda to grab her own stuff.

Twenty minutes later the cars were mostly unloaded, and everyone was inside picking their rooms and unpacking. Wayne came back to the Honda, where the only bags left were his brother's.

Brooke's spiteful plan didn't turn out to be very effective, because Gavin had been in the kitchen drinking beer while the others unpacked and couldn't have cared less about his bags. He had booze.

And if Gavin didn't screw him over, he'd be drinking some of it tonight, too.

The excitement of the thought helped Wayne find the strength to grab both of the duffle bags with one hand and carry them inside.

CHAPTER 17

BY THE TIME Ignacio was returning to the farmhouse from his errands downtown, it was nighttime. The full moon hung in the air like an over-sized balloon, and constellations glowed around it.

But the stars weren't the only thing that were glowing. The souls that lived on the campgrounds glowed, too. Some of them were nothing more than harsh orbs of light that floated between the cabins and the trees. They were too bright to look at for long periods of time, not that there was much to see in these amorphous souls to begin with. Others, though, Ignacio recognized. He recognized them very well, actually.

Because on some level, he'd brought them here. They were the souls of the victims he'd killed over the years—of the ones whose bodies had become a part of him when he ate them. The souls of his most recent prey, the young couple he'd ambushed last week, were here already.

Ignacio saw them as he walked through the campgrounds. The woman was underneath a tree, hugging her knees up to her chest. Tears ran down her eyes in streams that sparkled like glitter. They were tears of the damned, of the ones trapped in an existence that was neither living nor dead. The poor girl likely didn't know *where* she was, or even *what* she was anymore.

The man who was her boyfriend when they were living was out front of one of the big cabins. He had his hand on his chin, and he stared up at it like it was the greatest puzzle he'd ever seen. Really, though, the puzzle was somewhere else—on a plane Ignacio couldn't see.

In the living world there existed people who—like Ignacio—could get a peek into the afterlife and see spirits roaming about. But they couldn't see the world the spirits lived in. They were like a person who could open a blind and see what was outside but couldn't see anything beyond the scope of the window.

Ignacio didn't know any of this stuff, and didn't even know he had a special power, all he knew was that there were ghosts—*fantasmas*, as Mamá called them—and that he felt closer to his mother here than anywhere else in the world.

Ignacio finally made it past the part of the campgrounds where the spirits usually gathered. He sighed as he walked past the barn, glad to be away from the *fantasmas*. The truth was, if it weren't for Mamá, he wouldn't have stayed. But in this special spot in the woods, he could always feel Mamá's spirit all around him. Like she was hugging him, watching over him, kissing him all the time.

And that made putting up with the *fantasmas* worth it.

Ignacio went around to the back of the farmhouse first. There were several clothing lines set up in the open grass, but only a single vest made from the skin of Chad Richardson hung from one of the lines.

Ignacio touched the vest. It was still moist. It needed a few more hours in the sun before it would be good enough to wear.

He was disappointed, but at least that meant he would have something new to wear for Mamá's birthday tomorrow.

In the kitchen, he took out a big Ziploc bag from the fridge with meat in it that resembled chicken cutlets. The meat didn't belong to a bird at all, though; it was meat he'd chopped off Paige Silverstein's thighs. The chunks were nice and pink and healthy—Ignacio figured she must've been a jogger, and it was a good thing she'd tripped over that picnic table or she might've gotten away from him.

Ignacio put the meat into a baking dish, tossed it in oil, sprinkled salt and pepper on it, and topped it with onions, garlic, and rosemary. He turned the oven on and popped the dish into it.

Ignacio sat on the floor cross-legged and looked through the oven window. The lights in the farmhouse had dimmed because of the strain that turning the oven on put on the generator in the cellar. That was OK, though, because the dimness helped him watch the meat cook.

And that's exactly what he was going to do for the next forty minutes. He would watch the meat turn from pink to brown and crisp at the edges. He would watch the onions and garlic shrink as they released their juices. He would watch the whole meal cook without so much as blinking, because as Mamá had always said, he was a special boy with a special brain like no one else had.

CHAPTER 18

"About time," Fred said, sitting back on one of the chairs around the firepit. The kindling had finally caught fire, and the top of a long flame danced in the air.

Noelle, Fred, and Dalton were the only ones by the fire. Gavin and Fletcher were grilling up hotdogs and burgers for everyone on the cabin porch, while the girls were inside making margaritas with the mixer Vanessa had brought with her. The machine was a monstrosity that had been a point of contention as to who would bring it into the cabin, but ultimately Gavin had made Wayne lug it inside.

"It sure is secluded out here," Noelle said, looking through the trees.

"Yeah, I really thought Gavin was making up all of this stuff up about the cabin," Fred said, taking a drink of his beer.

"He's the type to stretch the truth, isn't he?" Dalton said.

Fred was annoyed with the guy already, because instead of helping him and Noelle get the fire going, he'd just sat in his chair playing some clone version of Bejeweled on his cellphone the whole time, so he was quick to jump to Gavin's defenses.

"He just likes to have fun."

"Ah," Dalton said, picking his cellphone up off his lap to resume his game. "Is that what that is?"

"He did a good job putting this trip together," Noelle said.

"Mm-hmm. Sure. That he did," Dalton said, getting up and leaving them to go inside the cabin.

"Jeez. What a party-starter," Fred said after he was out of earshot.

Noelle laughed, and looked over her shoulder at where Gavin and Fletcher were grilling. Gavin was shoving Fletcher backward, and pretending he was going to throw a hamburger with melting cheese on it at his face.

"You and I both know your friend isn't the easiest to get along with," she offered.

"What? Gav? He's…he's alright." Fred couldn't bring himself to fully commit to the lie. "Yeah, okay. You're right. He can be a bit much."

Noelle touched his shoulder. "You okay?"

Fred took in a deep breath. He couldn't keep his feelings from her, especially not if this was going to be the beginning of their relationship the way he hoped it would be. *It's time to let it all out, Fred Meyers.*

Now, it was him who looked over to where Gav and Fletcher were. It was a good distance between the firepit and the porch, so that neither duo was going to hear the other talking in a normal speaking voice. Gav and Fletch still seemed preoccupied with grilling and it didn't seem like they were coming over here anytime soon.

"It's just that we've kind of grown apart over the years," Fred said. "He's into the same stuff as he was back when we were high school."

"I see," Noelle said.

"He's still into 'getting pussy'—his words, not mine—and drinking, and smoking pot, and all that. I'm kind of growing out of that stuff, and at the same time I think growing out of our friendship."

Fred took a big swig of his beer and looked over at her. "Ah, sorry to be a buzzkill. Must be the beer."

Noelle shook her head. "I'm all ears if you've got more to say."

"No, I think that's it," Fred said, even though in his mind he was wondering how to lead the conversation where he wanted it to go. "I just hope he's alright after college. I've been... Ah, I'm going to sound like a dickbag, but I was thinking of distancing myself from him after this camping trip."

"Might be good for both of you, you know? Maybe losing a friend like you will make him realize he should get himself together."

"Yeah," Fred said. "I guess I've been feeling bad about it because I hadn't thought of it like that before."

"And you don't have to cut ties with him for good. You can always go back to being friends with him when you want... If he's open to that, of course."

Fred grinned at her. "I knew there was a reason I liked hanging out with you."

Noelle smiled at him. "Everything in life is temporary. Only thing that's forever is death."

Fred sat back in his chair, playing with the tab on the beer can. He kept pulling it up and letting it hit the top of the can, so it made a tiny metallic click. "I just hope in the end, he'll be okay."

CHAPTER 19

The walls of the room were covered with newspaper clippings. They were articles Ignacio had collected about his mother's murder in the weeks after it happened. In the center was the front-page article that'd been printed the day after it happened:

BELOVED NURSE KILLED IN HOME ROBBERY

Simple and to the point because anyone reading the local paper would recognize Federica Calderon even though they'd used a younger picture. Federica was sporting a 90s-style bob cut and holding an enormous eight-year-old Ignacio on her lap. Both were smiling, though Ignacio's lips were more turned crooked in an awkward grin. Like some sort of cheap doll's smile.

The article itself was mostly a celebration of Federica's life. It described her story as an immigrant from Mexico with no education who put herself through school to become a head nurse at the local hospital. It detailed how she did all this while being a single mother to a young boy.

The article didn't include Ignacio's name, only referring to him as "Federica's son" whenever it made mention of him. It also omitted that she was a single parent because her husband had been killed in Mexico due to a drug dealing incident and skipped over the episodes of prostitution to make ends meet. It was supposed to be a celebration, after all.

There was information about the day she'd been murdered, but since it was the article that was printed the day after, the details were scant. Federica had been stabbed to death when two robbers broke into her home in the middle of the day. After the two were caught, it was revealed that they were first-time, amateur kids who had no idea what they were doing. The youngest, a seventeen-year-old kid, stabbed Federica multiple times out of panic when she'd gone to the bedroom to investigate what the noises in the house were.

The article had gotten it all right up until that point, even the bit about her coming from the living room because when Ignacio found her body two hours later, the television had been on and playing novelas.

What they *didn't* get right was the part that said the robbers, for reasons unknown, had decapitated her corpse. They'd gotten that wrong, because that had been Ignacio's doing.

That day, a seventeen-year-old Ignacio had been working at the sandwich shop, where he was working the slicer machine. When he got home, he didn't notice anything wrong until he went up to his mother's bedroom. He walked past the kitchen without noticing the shattered window the robbers had used to come into the house. Or the rock sitting on the kitchen floor.

He found her stabbed multiple times—mostly in the chest, some in the shoulder—and didn't know what to do. He dropped to his knees, hugged her, and silently cried.

While he cried, he tried to think of a plan.

He remembered asking his father about the urn they always had in their house back in Mexico. His father told him it was his own mother's ashes—Ignacio's *abuelita*. Ignacio asked him what that meant, and his father told him that her body was burned after she died.

He was scared that someone would burn his mother's body now that she was dead, and he'd never see her beautiful face again. An idea dawned on him, and he went downstairs into the kitchen. He grabbed the good knife, the one Mamá always told him worked wonderful to cut the meat she used for their meals and cut his mother's head off.

He put her head into a plastic bag to keep the blood from dripping everywhere, then stored it in a box at the back of his closet. Then he called the cops, and the rest was taken over by them.

When they asked him questions about finding the body, he'd told two lies. First, they asked if he found the body without the head, and he said yes (which was why the article got that part wrong).

Second, they asked if he knew where the head was, and he said no. The cops searched the house after that, but they didn't find the head because they never checked in Ignacio's boxes, assuming it was all just clothes and other junk the robbers wouldn't have taken. They figured he was too stupid to tell lies, and there was plenty of evidence of a break in, so there was no reason for them to suspect him. Ignacio was glad about that, because he might've gotten in trouble if anyone found out that he had taken Mamá's head off her body.

But more important than that, the room he'd turned into a shrine in his mother's honor wouldn't be the same without it.

Federica Calderon's head was in the center of the room with the newspaper clippings. It was impaled on a long wooden stake attached to a cement base. Four run down nightstands Ignacio had found while dumpster diving surrounded her head like a makeshift *Dias de los Muertos* altar. The dressers had offerings on their surfaces for his mother's spirit: candles, a framed picture of Federica when she was younger, several snacks still in their wrappers (Ganzitos, Barritas, and a Paleta Payaso among them), hard candies, and flowers, and so on.

Someone who peered through the windows might see it and think there was some sort of Satanic ritual going on, but this was no place for the Devil. There was a plastic Jesus statue, poorly painted with a gaudy color selection, that towered behind Mamá's head. If that wasn't enough to keep the evil spirits away, the candles themselves were decorated with images of Jesus, the Virgin of Guadalupe, angels, and other Biblical figures.

Ignacio knelt down on a mat in front of Mamá's head. He took a box of matches out of his pocket and lit one. If Mamá were alive, she wouldn't let him have matches, but she wasn't. And honoring her, especially the day before her birthday, was more important than what Ignacio thought she would disapprove of.

He lit some of the candles, just enough for the room to be dimly lighted, then blew out the match. He slipped the box back into his pants, and from his other pocket pulled out a golden rosary. He always had this rosary on him, because it was Mamá's favorite one. She'd always taken it with her to mass on Sundays.

It'd been the most valuable thing Mamá owned, and ironically the one thing the robbers had left behind. They must have assumed it was only gold-colored, and instead took the other cheaper jewelry Federica had in her bedroom.

Ignacio leaned his elbows on the altar and touched his hands together in a prayer position with the rosary dangling between his palms. He closed his eyes and began reciting the *Our Father* in Spanish, the only prayer he could ever remember.

"*Padre nuestro, que estas en el cielo…*"

This was Ignacio's favorite part of every day, because while he prayed, he could feel Mamá closer to him than ever. Sometimes, he could even hear her sweet voice reciting the words with him.

CHAPTER 20

AFTER EATING BURGERS and hotdogs inside the cabin, the group was outside drinking and riding their buzzes by the firepit. They were all a little tired from the drive and unpacking, and the night seemed to be winding down.

Despite that the day had been hot and humid, the sun setting and the trees trapping the cool air of incoming breezes turned the night chillier than what they'd prepared for. The heat of the fire felt good against their skin and complemented the cold beers nicely.

Gathered here in front of this gorgeous cabin, surrounded by friends, music playing on the speaker by Fletcher's feet, it was almost too perfect of a summer night.

Something must be about to ruin it, Fred thought. Maybe a pair of glowing eyes in the brush would freak them out for a moment only to find out it was a racoon. Maybe they'd hear a strange sound in the distance. Maybe it'd start to rain—

"We should go skinny dipping," Gavin suggested, looking at the map spread out on his lap. "Says on the map there's a lake about a mile out from here."

Ah, there it is, Fred thought, trying not to smirk. It was almost like Gavin had read his thoughts. Or maybe more like he thought the group was too relaxed and wanted to change that. Yeah, that seemed more like Gavin Briggs' style.

Fletcher laughed, almost spitting out some beer. "You wanna go now? Like, tonight?"

"Yeah," Gavin said, jumping up to his feet, not caring that the map fell to the ground. "What, we came all the way out here just to sit around doing nothing?"

There was a murmur around the campfire from the others that to Fred, sounded sadly like agreement with Gavin. The truth was, he would have rather just spent this first night relaxing.

"We won't skinny dip, but we'll go," Brooke said from the other side of the campfire.

"I'm in," Fletcher said.

"You gonna skinny dip, though, right?" Gavin asked.

"Sure, man."

"My man," Gavin said to him. Then to Fred and Noelle, "What about you guys?"

"I'm coming!" Wayne called out before they had a chance to answer.

"Shut up," Gavin snapped at him.

Fred took in a deep breath and reluctantly said, "Yeah, yeah, I'll go. Noelle, you in?"

"Yeah," Noelle said. "Just like Gav said, what's the point of being out here if we're not going to explore the woods, right?"

"Oh no, Noelle. Don't go reinforcing this clown's ego," Fred protested.

Everyone laughed except for Dalton, who was sitting in a chair just outside of the circle formed by the others. "I think I'll be staying back."

He said it in a tone that made it sound like it was the generation's biggest reveal.

Gavin fought the urge to say, *no one asked you, dork*, but had to play nice. He had to play nice at least until he hooked up with Brooke. But after that? It was anything goes.

And he couldn't wait because Dalton was what Gavin would describe as a douchebag. The blue hair and the fake-rugged clothing he wore pissed him off the instant he'd met the guy back at his house. There was a lot of ammo Gavin was gathering up, and he couldn't wait to go off on him when the chance finally came.

For now, though, he just said, "You sure about that? It's gonna be spooky quiet without us here."

"Ah, that's alright. I'll enjoy the peace and quiet. Might be good for me. Would probably be good for you, too," Dalton said, crossing his legs.

"Yeah," Gavin said, noticing the underlying passive-aggressiveness in what he said. "It probably would be. But I like to party. Party hard."

"If we're going to go, let's go," Fred said, intervening before the two really started butting heads. "We're gonna have to grab flashlights before we head out."

They all looked out beyond the cabin when he said this. There were motion lights as well as some fixed lights outside the cabin that created about a twelve-foot radius of artificial light. But outside of this circle, besides the moonlight, everything was dark. No lights from neighboring cabins, no streetlamps, no car headlights, nothing. Just shadowy woods as far as they could see.

"Guys, maybe this isn't such a good idea." Brooke said.

"Realizing what I've already realized?" Dalton said, posturing up in his seat proudly.

"What're you talking about?" Gavin said.

"What if we…what if we get lost out there or something?" Brooke protested.

"We have the map," Gavin said, picking it off the ground and waving it in the air at her.

"Plus, there are probably markers on the trees," Fletcher guessed. "They always have those."

"I'll turn back with you if it starts to get too creepy," Vanessa said to her.

Their lack of concern tamed hers, and Brooke nodded. "Okay, fine… Alright, but I'm not skinny dipping, Gav."

They laughed again, all of them except Dalton. Then, they started inside the cabin to prepare for the hike.

Dalton watched the group hike into the woods from inside the cabin.

What a bunch of suckers, he thought.

They'd probably march straight into the belly of a beast if it would make them look cool online.

He was glad that he wasn't on any social media. No Facebook, no Instagram, no Twitter. The closest he came to any of that were the online writing forums where he posted his poetry. His cousin and her friends would know nothing about that. He assumed they had no artistic ability, no visions, no stories to tell.

Especially not that muscle dummy with the annoying little brother. A dark part of him hoped those two would be lost in the woods and wouldn't return. Not that he wanted them to die, per se, but he hoped they wouldn't come back to the cabin.

Let them find their way out of the woods and get back home, just never let me have to see them again, he thought, as the last of the group's flashlight was lost in the dark.

Dalton stood by the window for a few more minutes, staring out into the woods. The motion lights on the trees out front started to shut off, one by one. Each one that went out shrunk the radius of light surrounding the cabin by two or three feet, until eventually only the front porchlight was on.

A nervousness started to work its way into Dalton's stomach. It was dark out there, *truly* dark. Darker than he imagined it would've been. And he was out here alone. Suddenly, he wondered if maybe it would've been smarter to go hiking with them.

He gulped.

A motion light to the right of the cabin came on as something running through the bushes a few feet away activated it. Dalton looked, but whatever was out there was too quick. All he caught was a blur retreating into the darkness.

He took a big step back, keeping his eyes glued on the bushes.

Twigs snapped somewhere in that direction, sounding like fireworks going off in the quiet seclusion. Dalton thought he would piss his pants if it weren't for the terror. It was like his entire body—including his insides and blood—was frozen solid with fear.

Then, he saw the two beady eyes emerge from the bushes, followed by the snout that they sat on top of. He let out a short breath as the doe shyly came out of her hiding place and into the light. Dalton looked down at the front of his jeans and laughed in relief when he saw he really hadn't wet himself.

"Dalton, you giant fool!" he said to the empty cabin.

In the moment of uncertainty, his mind had started to imagine the most horrific thing would come out from behind the bushes. A three-headed monster or a ghost or something equally juvenile. It seemed that this kind of seclusion and darkness had a way of reawakening childish fears.

An idea popped into Dalton's mind for a poem, and he hurried over to his shared room in the cabin to grab his notebook. Something told him this would be the only peace and quiet he'd get on this trip.

And he was right. Just not in the way that he thought.

CHAPTER 21

IGNACIO WAS HAVING a nightmare. It was one he'd had many times before and he knew how it ended—badly, always badly. But he couldn't do anything about it, not even wake up from it. He could only ride along with it.

He was a little boy in the nightmare, maybe six years old. A big six year old, but nowhere near as big as he was as an adult.

He was coming home from school. The curtains were all pulled down in the house. There were noises, moans, coming from Mamá's bedroom. The room's door was slightly open, enough that light escaped from the gap and lit the hallway leading to the bedroom with candlelight, but not open enough to see what was happening inside. The air was stale and smelled like a mixture of sweat, Mamá's perfume, and sex (although Ignacio didn't know what that was, then or now).

"Mamá..." Ignacio said, walking down the hallway toward the bedroom. "*Eres tu, Mamá?*"

He heard no reply. Only more moans coming from Mamá, and the bed squeaking.

Ignacio continued plodding down the hallway. With each step he took, the hallway seemed to stretch out longer and longer, the door getting further and further from him.

He called out to his mother again, but there was no reply.

Ignacio picked his pace up, almost jogging down the hallway, and finally reached the door. Mamá's rhythmic huffs of breath between the louder moans made him stop.

Was someone hurting her?

(No. He knew how it ended, he knew what was behind the door, but his dream version didn't... and Ignacio couldn't control anything in the nightmare, not even the thoughts in his head.)

He pushed the door open and saw Mamá on her back.

Her legs were in the air, with black tentacles wrapped around her ankles. The tentacles belonged to a humanoid creature as dark as a moonless night.

Mamá's head was upside down, hanging off the edge of the bed. Blood ran down her neck and into her mouth from a deep slash across her throat. She smiled when she saw Ignacio, showing him her blood-covered teeth.

"Hello, *hijo*," she said, licking her lips clean even though the blood kept coming in a torrential downpour, quickly covering her mouth again. "You're home early."

At the sound of her voice, the tentacled creature lifted its head up from out of her crotch. "*GET OUT!*"

Ignacio had gone from being a five-year-old boy to a full-grown adult as he'd walked down the hallway. In real life, he'd been too little, too powerless to do anything about the men he'd seen making Mamá moan, but in here, in this dream, he was big and powerful like in real life. He could fight the monster off and save Mamá.

This was his second chance.

Ignacio jumped at the monster, both hands out in front of him, ready to rip the monster's head off. One of the creature's tentacles let Mamá's leg go and shot out, grabbing him by the throat. The tentacle stretched out, pushing Ignacio back, and slammed him into a wall. All the air came rushing out of his lungs.

Still pinning him against the wall, the creature lifted Ignacio into the air like he was weightless.

Over the creature's shoulder, he saw Mamá was still laying on the bed with a big, bloody smile on her face. Her head began to wiggle around, and the slash across her throat opened wider. Blood dripped out of it faster, soaking the carpet at the edge of the bed even more.

Ignacio grabbed at the tentacle. It was wet and slimy, but strong. He was powerless against this creature—just as he'd been powerless in real life against the men who made Mamá moan.

"*YOU HAVE NO POWER*," the creature barked.

Ignacio closed his eyes and screamed.

He awoke screaming in real life. He was covered in sweat. Mamá's rosary was clutched in his hands the way he'd fallen asleep holding it.

Another nightmare. Ignacio went into fetal position, holding the rosary tight to his body with one hand and sucked the thumb of the other.

The room was pitch black, the kind of darkness that seemed to swallow you.

He was lonely. He missed Mamá.

Ignacio waited for his eyes to adjust to the darkness, then got out of the bed and changed out of his pajamas. He was going out to the barn to visit his Barbie as he often did when he felt lonely.

CHAPTER 22

*C*OUPLE NEVER RETURNS *from 'most secluded' cabin in PA.* Fred hadn't thought about the headline since they were at the gas station until now. They'd been having too much fun at the cabin, but in these dark woods the eeriness was beginning to outweigh the fun. Especially now that they'd traveled far enough away from the cabin that they couldn't see it anymore.

"Why are you all so quiet?" Gavin said from the front of the group. Despite his question, he too had gone quiet after a few minutes of whistling when everyone else's chatter had stopped about fifteen minutes ago. He turned around to face them but kept walking backward. "You'd think someone died or something."

"We're just trying to enjoy the hike," Brooke said to him. "Watch where you're walking, dork! You don't want to trip out here!"

"Ah, whatever," Gavin said, throwing his hands in the air, but she was right, and he faced forward again. There'd been a few root knots and rocks jutting out of the earth like giant knuckles that he'd already almost stumbled over. Walking backward out here at night wasn't the wisest decision.

The exchange between Gavin and Brooke sprouted conversations among the others. The path they hiked was only wide enough for two people walking side by side. Noelle was next to Fred, and noticed how pale he'd gotten. Maybe it was just the way the moonlight reflected off him, but she wanted to make sure.

She leaned in close to him. "Hey, Fred. You okay?"

Fred nodded. "Yeah, I'm alright."

But the truth was, he couldn't stop thinking about the missing people reports in these parts. It would never happen to them, of course. Because they were being careful, following the orange reflectors marking the trail to the lake.

What if the couple had been careful, too? he argued with himself, wishing he would've read that damn article after all.

How long could the article have taken him to read? Twenty minutes? He would gladly exchange twenty minutes of lost sleep last night to know what happened to that couple right now.

Fred felt his heart beating faster in his chest, and suddenly the air felt too thick to breathe. Like he'd been shoved into a vat of molasses or something.

Then, he felt Noelle's soft hands wrap around his arm. She leaned her head onto his shoulder, and he caught a whiff of her hair—some sort of floral scent, lavender maybe—and in an instant everything was okay again.

"You're not spooked, are you, Fred Meyers?" she said, turning her head to look at him with almond-colored eyes. "Because I'll protect you from the fear bees if you are."

"Fear bees?" Fred smiled.

She grinned. "I used to tell my sister when she was real little that there were bees that could smell fear. And whenever she was afraid of something, I'd say 'the fear bees will come if you don't stop being afraid.' It worked to help her get over being scared of the dark and stop peeing her bed."

Fred laughed. "That's cute."

Noelle gave his arm a tight squeeze before breaking away from him. "You better make sure you're not calling them to us, Fred Meyers."

"Uh, yeah. I'll make sure I'm not."

The group fell silent again as they followed their flashlight beams through the hike. They walked a good fifteen yards or so like this, until Gavin stumbled on a big root from an oak tree he didn't see. He shot his arms out in front of him to keep from faceplanting right into the dirt.

The others laughed, but Fred noticed they didn't laugh the way they had back at the cabin. Or even at the beginning of this nighttime hike. They laughed like they knew this was a bad idea.

If fear bees were real, Fred thought, they'd have already called an entire swarm on themselves.

CHAPTER 23

Out here in these desolate woods, it was easy for anyone to pick up on sounds that disturbed the natural quietness. Ignacio, however, wasn't just anyone. He was born a special boy (as Mamá always told him) with super hearing abilities, which meant he could practically hear anything going on out here if he focused hard enough.

Human voices were different, though. They were distinct enough, and rare enough out here, that they always perked up his senses.

That's what his ears were picking up on now. Voices in the trees. He stopped, halfway to the barn from the farmhouse, and listened closely. Now that he was outside the grove of trees that surrounded the farmhouse, he could hear the voices better. There were several of them, walking through a path that wasn't too far away.

He knew exactly which path it was, and the shortest way through the woods to it, because Ignacio knew these woods better than anyone. He knew them better than even the animals did.

His brain was slow, or so he was told, but it could memorize the geography of places perfectly.

Changing directions, he headed toward the voices. He wanted to see if there was anything worth hunting down.

Ignacio crouched down behind a thick bush. Using two heavy fingers he separated some branches to get a better view of the trail. The hikers hadn't made the turn to come into his view yet, but he could hear them in the distance, so he blew out his lantern.

Now, he heard them better. Their voices had an unsteady, nervous quake to them—a hint of fear. It excited Ignacio, and he was ready to jump out and attack them right then and there, but Varias Caras took over before he could do that and he stayed put.

We don't have a weapon, tonto.

That's right. He'd been on his way to the barn, not out to hunt. He didn't have anything except his hunting knife on him, and that wouldn't do much with this many of them. He needed something more powerful for those numbers.

The hikers came into his view. A muscled-up guy in a sleeveless shirt led the group. Behind him, six others marched in a haphazard bunch.

There were three boys besides the leader. Two who looked in their early twenties, and a third one who was much younger than anyone else in the group. He looked like a shaggy-haired teenage version of the muscled-up guy.

Then there were three girls; A tall blond with a confident walk that made Ignacio nervous, a smaller girl in jeans and hiking boots and silver hair, and a third girl with caramel-colored skin.

This one… This was the one that caught his attention.

She was beautiful. Hispanic, with long hair, thick eyebrows, and plump lips.

"Mamá…?" Ignacio whispered.

Ignacio watched the campers coming toward him. Each of their flashlights shone over him as they rounded the path, but just as he thought would happen, they didn't see him. They were too focused on following the bend in the trail.

They walked past him, one by one, but he couldn't keep his eyes off the Hispanic girl.

Yes. She looked like Mamá. Like Mamá when she was young, he thought, remembering the family album back in his bedroom.

He caught a glimpse of her calves flexing as she walked by his hiding spot.

Ignacio licked his lips, feeling the roughness of the mask on the bottom of his tongue. She excited him in a way he'd never felt before. He wanted her. Needed her.

It didn't matter how many there were to try to stop him from taking her. He would have her.

The group marched past him and were swallowed up by the darkness. He could still hear their whispers in the distance. There was a faint sound of laughter—one of them was *her* laughter. He was sure of it because it made his heart flutter.

"I—I want," he muttered.

Not tonight. Varias Caras said to him. *A good hunter waits for the perfect opportunity.*

Ignacio smacked himself on the head to shake the urge of chasing her down.

He echoed Varias Caras' message. "Not tonight."

He stood up from his crouch, and then backed up into the shadows. Mamá's lookalike had gotten away, for now.

CHAPTER 24

The light from outside cut through the barn like a saber, stirring Nadine awake. She opened her eyes—slowly, always slowly so the sudden brightness wouldn't damage her eyes. There was always pain, but that she couldn't do anything about.

Varias Caras pulled the door closed and started toward Nadine. At night, there was almost no light inside the barn, so the only way she could track his movements was by the lantern.

"Good evening, *bella*!" he said, dropping a satchel in front of her.

Varias Caras lit the torches hanging on the wall with a match, putting this part of the barn in an orange glow. He was wearing a mask she'd never seen before. The mask was old. Not just in the sense that the material was old, which it was, but also that the person whose face it had been had died at an elderly age. It looked like an old woman's face. There was even poorly applied makeup on it.

Varias Caras crouched down and unzipped the satchel. One by one, like a kid counting to make sure all his marbles were in the bag, he took out the makeup supply. A compact, some brushes, and a gold lipstick sat in a neat row in front of him.

If it'd been an appropriate time for humor, Nadine would've laughed at the lipstick. It was like a child's idea of what a woman would use. The whole layout was, really, but the lipstick was the kicker.

Varias Caras looked up at her, noticing Nadine staring at the mask. He rocked back on his heels and fell onto his ass. "Want to hear about mask?"

Nadine didn't say anything, just continued to stare at him. As comforting as it was to have someone speak to her, she didn't like talking back to him.

But as he often did, Varias Caras took her silence as meaning, yes, and went into his story.

"I save money some years ago." Varias Caras bobbed his head with each syllable. "Fly to Mexico."

He also paused and took in a deep breath every other sentence. It reminded Nadine of one of her third graders with asthma, a small boy named Samuel, who would stand with her during recess and tell her about his bug collection or his toys because he couldn't play with the other kids. The thought of that boy, and the rest of her third graders, made her want to cry.

But she didn't have the energy to. Not right now, anyway.

Varias Caras continued. "I visit abuelita's grave. Start digging. Guy working the graveyard shoots at me. Almost hits me with bullet."

If only he would have killed you, Nadine thought.

"I return next day." He hacked through the air with his hand as if it were a blade. "Cut head off. Maybe same guy. Maybe not. Not sure…"

Varias Caras paused to suck in breath. "I take abuelita's face off for mask…then return body to grave. In Mexico, we respect our elders."

Finishing the story, he went back into a crouch. He picked up the compact and opened it. The powder inside was old and dry, and he had to press the brush hard against it to get the makeup to stick to it.

"Hold still, and nothing bad happens," Varias Caras warned.

The irony of it made Nadine glance at the ends of her legs, where smooth, blackened nubs were instead of her feet. The first night he'd captured her, he'd cut her feet off so she "couldn't run away" and had cauterized the wounds with a piece of metal he heated up with a blowtorch so "they wouldn't hurt and bleed too much." Nadine supposed there *were* worse things he could still do to her, but the irony of his choice of words was hard to ignore.

Using the brush, he applied the blue eyeshadow onto her face. It got everywhere because the brush was too small for his large fingers to handle with any sort of dexterity. He dipped the brush into the red makeup next, and then applied that on her face.

Nadine didn't need a mirror to know the job was sloppy. She could feel the dry powder caked in swatches all across her face. It went from her cheeks and up to her hairline, and probably was in her hair, too.

Done with the compact, he closed it and stuffed it and the brush back into the satchel. Then he picked up the gold lipstick. He took the cap off, revealing that the actual makeup inside was cherry-red. It didn't really make much sense given the circumstances, but Nadine felt some sort of relief at this.

Varias Caras traced her lips with the precision of a toddler trying to color inside the lines. The lipstick got as high up as her nostrils and as low as her chin.

Ignacio (this was all Ignacio, Varias Caras was gone) sat back with a big, proud smile as he admired his work. After a few seconds of that, he gathered up all the supplies and stashed them in the satchel. His hand came out with a small mirror in it that he held up to Nadine.

The application of the makeup was awful, but even worse than that was the gaunt face staring back at her. Her skin was paper thin, tinged yellow, and stretched tightly over her protruding bones. Her eyes looked sunken into her head. She could see dark shadows around them in the spots where the blue-red dust wasn't covering. The hair on her head was stringy, and greasy, and patches of it were missing. Nadine wanted to scream, because it was like staring at the face of a monster, but she didn't because she didn't want to anger Varias Caras.

Besides, it wasn't a monster she was looking at. It was herself.

Ignacio moved the hand mirror away from her and put it in the satchel with the rest of the beauty products.

"You like? Now, we both pretty," Ignacio said, smiling.

Nadine watched him return from the Butcher Room with a large cardboard box with pieces of metal jutting out the top of it. She watched Varias Caras carry the box several feet down the same wall Nadine was chained to, just barely still under the glow of the torches, and set it down.

Varias Caras went through the box, chucking the pieces of metal into a pile in front of him that looked like nothing but a bunch of scraps. Then he pulled a chain out of the bag, and Nadine realized what was happening.

It was a disassembled set of restraints, just like the ones keeping her.

The second chain clanked as it hit the top of the pile. Varias Caras got up, went over to the shelf where he kept his chainsaw, and grabbed a hammer and a box of nails. He returned to the wall, picked up a metal part, and started nailing it to the wall.

He spoke to Nadine between bangs. "Tomorrow Mamá's birthday. I bring another Barbie back. We have party."

Bang. Bang. Bang.

"Maybe have to let you go," he said, shaking his head. "I cannot take care of two Barbies. You understand?"

Bang. Bang.

Another girl? Oh God, he's bringing someone else to this barn. The realization broke Nadine's heart in a way she didn't know was possible. He was going to capture another innocent person, and subject them to…*this*. Someone out there, in the world Nadine was sure she'd never see again, was living the last moments of their life before being brought into this hell. And she was powerless to help the girl—couldn't even warn her about it.

Nadine surprised herself by sobbing. The sobs came out so loud they could be heard over Varias Caras' hammering.

He stopped, and without looking at her he asked, "Why are you sad?"

She didn't respond, just continued to cry. Ignacio dropped the hammer on the floor. His mind completely changed tracks, and he went over to Nadine, crouching in front of her again.

"Why do you cry?" he asked again.

Nadine wiped at her eyes with the back of her hands. Her chains clinked.

"Nothing… nothing…" she muttered.

She'd been trapped here long enough to know her captor's temperaments. She could feel his mood change without having to see his facial expressions. As large as he was physically, the energy he exuded was just as large, and right now, she could feel him getting angry. That seemed to be his default response for not understanding things, to get angry at the situation.

Nadine tried to get ahold of herself in hopes of stopping the impending anger, but she couldn't. This was too much.

"You stop! You stop crying!" Varias Caras jumped up to his feet. He started stomping around like a child who'd just had his video games taken away from him. "Stop! Stop!"

The more he screamed and commanded her to stop, the harder it was for her to comply. Unlike a child, his temper tantrums scared her. Nadine felt the ground underneath her shaking, and she cried harder.

"Stop! STOP!" He covered his ears with his hands and shook his head to muffle the sound. The noise was too much, and he was too uncomposed to control his hearing sensitivity like he usually could. "YOU STOP RIGHT NOW!"

But that didn't work, and he decided it was time to give her a reason to cry. Like Papá had done to him.

He pulled out the knife from his back pocket and crouched down in front of Nadine. Ignacio grabbed a handful of hair from the back of her head and brought her face inches from his. She was so close to him she could smell the musk of the leather mask.

"Stop or I cut!" Varias Caras warned.

Nadine nodded, sniffled, and stopped crying. She'd used up all her energy by now, anyway.

The quiet in the barn returned, and Varias Caras waited to see if it was a permanent thing or if she was going to start up again.

After a minute or so, he was satisfied. He stood up and put the knife back in his pocket. He started back to finish setting up the restraints.

Nadine looked at the handle of the knife sticking out from his back pocket. If only she could get her hands on it… But no, he was too far away for her to even attempt anything like that. Besides, where would she go? She had no idea where she was, and with no practice moving quickly on the nubs of her legs, she might never get out of the woods alive.

There was nothing she could do except sit here, listening to him build the capture device for his next victim.

Bang. Bang. Bang.

CHAPTER 25

As it turned out, Gavin managed to convince Brooke, Vanessa, and Fletcher to skinny dip when they got to the lake. Fred and Noelle resisted his silly idea, and Wayne was forbidden from joining them, so the three of them were sitting on a towel on the lake bank.

"Hurry up! It's nice and cool in here!" Gavin yelled out at the girls who were still in the bushes.

He was the only one in the water, floating like a stray buoy in the middle of the lake. The moon hung over the trees, bigger and brighter than any of them had ever seen it. Its light turned the surface of the lake almost mirror-like, reflecting the surrounding willow trees on its rippling water.

"Hold on! Gosh, so impatient," Brooke said, but the girls were laughing.

The truth was, they were all relieved to be out of the woods and now they were in better spirits.

"You trying to catch some flies there, bud?" Noelle said to Wayne, who was staring at the girls with widened eyes.

He couldn't see anything from this angle, but the fact that he was this close to naked college girls was unbelievable enough for him. Noelle's words only managed to half-snap him out of his trance and he continued to stare at the girls as he jumped to his feet.

"Uhh... I gotta go take a leak," he said, and started for the trees without waiting for a response.

"Can you tell he's Gav's brother?" Fred said.

They both watched him disappear into the shadows. And disappear was exactly the word they were both thinking, because once the darkness swallowed his flashlight's beam, there was no more trace of Wayne Briggs.

"You think you should go with him?" Noelle asked.

Before Fred could answer, Gavin yelled at Fletcher and drew their attention that way. At the last second, Fletcher had chickened out and was coming into the lake with his underwear on.

"Nah, I think he'll be okay," Fred said. "The Briggs brothers are loud enough that if he screams, we'll hear him all the way out here."

Noelle laughed, and a silence fell between them. But out here, underneath a willow tree by the lake, there was nothing awkward about it.

"It's so pretty out here," Noelle said after a minute or so.

She was staring up at the starry sky, a view that often stole the breaths of the city-dwellers and suburbanites that ventured out this far into the woods.

"Yeah," Fred agreed, staring up at the moon looming over them. "It's almost as pretty as you."

As soon as the words escaped his mouth, his face flushed red. He was sure Noelle was going to laugh at his lame attempt at flirting, but she surprised him by giggling.

"Oh, is that so?" she said. "Is Fred Meyers hitting on me?"

Flustered, Fred straightened up and tried to sober. "Uh, yeah. Maybe."

Great recovery, idiot. The voice scolding him in his head sounded a lot like Gav's.

Noelle slapped him on the shoulder. "It's too bad you didn't make a move sooner."

Fred felt his heart sunk and his balls shrivel up into his body, so much so that they seemed to be meeting in the pit of his stomach. "Huh?"

"I'm kind of seeing someone… We decided to make things official just yesterday, before our camping trip. I'm sorry, Fredster." Noelle saw his spirits were down and pecked him on the cheek. It didn't do anything to pick him up, but it was worth the try. "We can still be friends, right?"

You snooze, you lose. Gavin's voice again. Then his own: *God fucking damnit.*

"Friends," Fred muttered. "Yeah, friends."

Friends forever.

Wayne couldn't see shit even from where he was now. The bushes covered the girls up completely.

He got his hopes up when they started for the lake, but they ran too fast for him to get any details. The girls jumped into the lake and swam into parts deep enough that their bodies were obscured by the water.

Bummer.

The best he got was the colors of their nipples, and tried to masturbate to that, but couldn't focus. There were too many distractions out here. Gavin kept yelling and every time the wind rustled the bushes, he was sure it was someone about to sneak up on him and see what he was doing.

Oh well. He'd wait until they were back at the cabin to rub one out.

Since he was already holding onto his dick, he figured he may as well take a piss. Wayne finished with that, then started back to join the others.

They got tired of swimming twenty minutes later. The skinny dippers headed back to the bank, dressed in wet clothes since the only towel they'd brought was the one Noelle and Fred were sitting on. They stood up and handed it over to the girls, each using one end of the towel to dry their hair.

Gavin sensed something going on between Noelle and Fred—he'd known Fred long enough to know all his tells—and he made a mental note to remember to ask him about it later.

"Well, well, you guys missed out on a rad experience," Gavin said to them.

"Yeah, wet socks sure are an experience," Fred replied.

"How'd the mosquitos treat you two?"

"Okay, boys. Settle down," Brooke said. She picked the map off the ground and started leading them to the trail they'd come from.

"Wait, where's Wayne?" Gavin said.

As if the question summoned him, Wayne emerged out from the bushes. "I'm here!"

"Oh," Gavin said, then pointed at the front of his cargo shorts. "Your fly's down."

The girls all laughed.

Wayne's face burned hot with embarrassment, and he looked down at the front of his shorts. Indeed, his zipper was all the way down, and even worse the gold seemed to be glowing underneath the moonlight.

"Uh, uh—shit—" he said, fumbling to zip it up. "I was taking a piss!"

But no one cared about his explanation. They had all moved on from the moment and were packing up. As reluctant as they were to hike through the darkened path again, they were ready to get back to the cabin.

CHAPTER 26

A FEW MILES AWAY from Lakewood Cabin there was a smaller, less extravagant—though just as secluded—cabin in the woods. Emeril opened the rickety cabin's door, half expecting the squeaking hinges to rip right off the wall.

That didn't happen. Instead, he was greeted by a blast of musk and dampness that seemed to have been trapped for far too long.

"Whoa, dear Lord," Emeril said, swatting the air away from his face as if that would somehow combat the smell. "Smells like someone's wet shoe."

Molly came up from behind him, holding the tripod in her arms. "Beggars can't be choosers, Emeril."

"I suppose that's true," he said, flipping the switch on the wall next to him up.

A bare bulb hanging from the middle of the cabin turned on, and Emeril went inside. Molly walked past him and set the tripod on a table in the kitchen. The table was so old she was worried for a second it might turn to dust.

She turned to Emeril, who was inspecting a hole in the roof. "Making you wish we would've called Andy Cameron for one of his cabins?"

"I think dealing with him once was enough," Emeril said, smiling at her.

It was true, but Emeril also knew this was the only cabin within distance of the location they were scoping out. There was a reason Lakewood Cabin was billed as the 'most secluded cabin in PA.' Besides this dilapidated cabin, their other options were all places to set up tents.

All things considered, Emeril felt better with four walls between them and the dark woods outside. Even if the structure looked about ready to collapse with a strong gust, he'd take his chances on that. Cannibals or no cannibals out there, these parts were the stomping grounds of wild animals.

Molly was thinking the same thing and stopped at the doorway when a question she'd been meaning to ask dawned on her. "We're going to these locations during the day tomorrow, right?"

"Yes," Emeril said. "Why?"

"No reason," Molly said. "Just, maybe we'd have a better idea of where we're going during the day, is all."

"Mm-hmm," Emeril agreed. "Also, less dangerous."

"It's like you read my mind."

"Yeah," Emeril said, suddenly feeling like he needed to sit. He settled into one of the chairs in the kitchen area.

"You okay, Emeril?"

Emeril nodded, and put his palm up in a gesture that said, "don't worry about me." But to Molly, he looked like he was in the middle of having a heart attack. She stepped closer to him and reached out to him.

"No, please!" he barked.

Molly stopped and brought her hand back like Emeril might take a bite out of it. "You sure you're okay?"

He was breaking out in a sweat now, but he nodded to Molly. He needed to hold strong… "C-can you just get me some water?"

"Yeah, sure," Molly said and charged out of the cabin. She grabbed a water bottle from one of the packs they had in the back of the Subaru and hurried back inside.

Something was going on with him… something strange. Something that didn't feel physical or mental or even physiological, but otherworldly. Like an earthquake was happening inside of him. Emeril could feel his insides trembling. They seemed to move unrhythmically and independent of one another.

He grabbed the edge of the table to steady himself. It didn't do him any good, but whatever was happening ceased in the same moment. His breathing came back to him. Emeril shook his head hard and felt the beads of sweat roll down his face.

He focused and realized that he felt lighter than ever. Like a weight had been lifted off his chest.

Molly came back into the cabin, unscrewing the cap on the water bottle in her hands. Relief washed the concern off her face as she saw the color returning in Emeril's face.

"Here," she said, handing him the water bottle anyway.

Emeril took it and gulped almost half the bottle down in one go. With his forearm, he wiped at his mouth. "Thank you, Molly."

"You okay?"

He nodded.

"You sure? Maybe we should go to a hospital—"

"No, no. Must've been the humidity of the place," he lied.

"Okay," Molly said, not entirely convinced. "Yeah, it is muggy in here."

She looked him over once more, then started back outside. "I'm going to unpack the rest of our stuff."

"I'll be there in a second," Emeril promised.

Molly went out of the cabin, leaving him in the kitchen by himself again.

Emeril was feeling odd still, but he had to hold strong. They were close to uncovering something in these woods. Now that his mind was clearer, he realized that's what the odd sensation he experienced had been. Something in these woods was touching a hidden sense—something Emeril only presumed he had until now.

That's why he couldn't describe what it was to himself, because he was like a newborn seeing light for the first time or taking in his first breath out of the womb. More than ever now, he knew the supernatural was real, and they were on the verge of finding concrete evidence to back up years of his presumptions.

He had literally felt it trembling through his body a moment ago.

He had to hold strong. He was close to catching his white whale.

CHAPTER 27

"WHAT'RE YOU DOING up so early, Fredster?" Gavin said, joining Fred on the porch. They were both leaning against the banister now.

"Oh, uh, just couldn't sleep. What about you?"

Gavin popped the tab on his beer can and took a sip. "The wind kept smacking a branch against a window all night. I was ready to go cut that fucking tree down last night."

They both looked at one another, and both burst out laughing. Gavin had made a big deal about staying in the master bedroom himself, since this whole camping trip was his idea and the rest owed it to him and all that. The others, not wanting to argue with him, let him have it even though it meant sharing rooms with the others. In a cosmically funny twist, it turned out to be the most disruptive room to sleep in.

"Karma gets you once again," Fred said.

"Whatever," Gavin responded. He took another drink of his beer and let the quiet between them clear the humorous mood before changing the subject. "You gonna tell me the real reason you're up early? Something happened by the lake, didn't it? With Noelle?"

Fred shifted his weight to his other foot and rubbed the back of his neck. "You going to give me shit if I tell you?"

Gavin scanned his face, and saw Fred was legitimately concerned about it. He shook his head. "No—I mean, maybe. I'm a dick, you know? That's kind of my thing."

Fred laughed, but there was nothing behind it. Gavin punched him on the arm playfully and said, "No, I won't laugh at you. Tell me."

"Ah, man. I feel really stupid about this. You were right, though. I waited too long. She has a boyfriend—or, she's 'seeing someone' as she put it."

"Ah, Fredster," Gavin said, putting his arm around his shoulders. "All things end. Good, bad. Neither. They all end. Eventually, everything ends. Don't you ever forget that."

Now it was Fred's turn to feel the forces of cosmic irony, because Noelle had said something to that effect about him and Gav's friendship just yesterday. If he didn't know any better, he would've thought the two conspired this behind his back.

Of course, that wasn't what happened. It was a lot simpler than that: Time passes, and things change. Everyone knows that, even if it's easy to forget sometimes.

The only thing that's certain is death.

"When you're right, you're right, Gav," Fred said to him.

They went quiet for a good while after that, and just watched the sunrise in the distance and listened to the morning birds twittering in the trees.

Focus... Focus... Fletcher told himself, trying to imagine the dart flying across the room and hitting the bullseye. *If you can imagine it, you can achieve it.*

He launched the dart...and missed completely. The dart struck the wood paneling behind the target, bounced off, and fell to the floor.

"Man! You suck!" Gavin laughed from the wall he was leaning against.

He was bored of beating Fletcher at darts, so he headed out of the room to see if the girls were done cooking breakfast.

By himself now, Fletcher was done with the game too. He went to fetch the dart behind the entertainment stand where he saw it bounce.

Fletcher ducked down to get the dart but stopped when he saw a crumpled piece of paper stuck between the furniture and the wall. What he could see of it was colorful, with lines going every which way. There was a strange allure to it, and he stuck his hand in the gap and took it out.

He uncrumpled it. Dust came out between the folded crevices. Fletcher blew on the map he was staring at to clear the dust off it.

The graphics on this map were in an older style, but it was almost exactly the same as the one they'd used last night. In fact, the YOU ARE HERE arrow even pointed to Lakewood Cabin. Everything else was there, too: Willow Lake, the trail they'd used to get there, even a giant boulder covered in graffiti they passed was on there as a landmark.

The biggest difference, and the part that drew Fletcher's eyes, was that someone had drawn in a series of tiny cabins with a Sharpie. Over the cabins was the name CAMP LAKEWOOD. This was all done over where the map originally had nothing but trees.

"Weird," Fletcher said under his breath.

He started to fold the map up and put it in his pocket when he heard feet shuffling into the room.

"Yo," Gavin said. He stopped at the doorway. "You okay?"

"Yeah, yeah," Fletcher said, trying to straighten up. "Just can't find the dart is all."

"It's right there," Gavin said, pointing by one of the entertainment system's legs where a fluorescent green dart tail was poking out of. "You sure you're alright?"

Fletcher forced out a short laugh. "I think maybe I hit the bong a little too hard this morning."

"Never that, bro." Gavin smiled at him.

"I'll be alright," Fletcher said, relieved he'd bought the lie.

"Well, the girls got breakfast ready. Breakfast burritos. Hurry your ass up or I'll scarf down yours, too." Gavin laughed, then left the room.

Fletcher grabbed the dart from underneath the entertainment system, then put it in the metal bucket with all the others.

Before heading back, he took the map out of his pocket and looked it over again. He'd half expected the map to have disappeared from his pocket or disintegrated, but it hadn't. It was still there, mysterious and oddly drawn-in cabins and all.

He wasn't sure why, but it felt like he'd found some sort of hidden treasure map. The feeling was similar to when he discovered a new indie band he liked, and he would listen to their discography before telling anyone to check them out, so could remain the "expert" on the subject. It was a douchey thing, but the same thing was happening here.

He wanted to gander over the map a few times, take in all the details. Maybe get a current map and compare so that he could point out the differences to the others when he finally showed them this retro map.

There wasn't much of a point to this, because really, no one would care. But in the moment, it felt right. For a second, he wondered if it actually *was* the pot he'd smoked making him feel like this.

Then his stomach grumbled, reminding him of Gav's threat to eat his burrito if he didn't hurry. Putting the map back in his pocket, he raced out to meet the others on the deck.

CHAPTER 28

Nadine was stirred awake by the sound of the barn door rolling open. She sat up, shielding her eyes from the bit of sunlight coming into the barn. It was an odd daytime visit today.

Varias Caras walked through the barn and set his camo bag down in front of her. The mask he was wearing today was a man's face. It was cracked and dry and looked ready to fall apart. There were stitches running from the top right side of the forehead that went diagonally down to the left cheek, which suggested it already had fallen apart before. The sewing was done so poorly it looked like a long centipede crawling on the face.

"Good morning!" he said happily. "Makeup look pretty still. Pretty, pretty."

He bent down and planted a slurping kiss on her cheek.

Nadine's stomach turned, but she was thankful that her captor was as petulant as he was. He had no sexual desires, and didn't do anything beyond kissing her, because all he wanted from women was platonic companionship. Nothing more. The problem was, he went about achieving it in the worst ways possible.

Varias Caras unzipped the bag and took out a red dress from it. It was long, with frills on the ends of it and on the sleeves. Nadine wouldn't have ever picked it out herself and worn it, in fact, Stephen probably would have made fun of her for wearing something like it, but it was undoubtedly a pretty dress.

"Mamá's favorite dress," Varias Caras explained to her, holding it up in the air so that the dress flowed down to its length. "You like?"

Nadine nodded. She saw his fat lips curl up into a smirk.

"Good." He got up.

He put the dress on the shelf where he kept the chainsaw and other tools, then grabbed a hose off one of the bottom levels. He screwed the hose into a faucet that was only a few feet from Nadine, then walked over to her, leaving the hose coiled like a snake on the ground for the moment.

"Bring other girl here today. Have party for Mamá's birthday," Varias Caras told her. "Have to clean you first. You understand?"

"Yes," Nadine said.

"I take clothes off now," he said.

He always announced that he was going to strip her clothes off before he did it. It always came off like he was apologizing for it.

Deep down inside, Nadine appreciated the decency. It made her sick with herself to see any shred of humanity in this monster, but maybe that was what the mind did in these situations. It looked for any forms of consolation to outweigh the horrors.

"Up, up," Varias Caras said, reaching around the waistband of her shorts. Nadine complied, and used her stubs to raise her buttocks so he could slip the gym shorts off her.

He never put any underwear on her (either because he didn't want to bother with the extra work or because he didn't understand the function of it, Nadine wasn't sure), so she settled back on the ground bare ass. The floor felt ice cold against her skin.

Next, he started undoing the cuffs around her wrists and her neck. This wasn't as freeing as it may have seemed, because he undid the locks with one hand and pointed a knife at her with the other.

Often when he was changing her shirt, she thought about wrestling the knife from his grip, but the scenarios played out like movie snapshots in her head with completely different outcomes.

In one scenario, she would take the knife from him and be quick enough to slash his throat open. Varias Caras would fall to his death instantly. She'd take the keys from his pockets and unshackle herself, then get out of this demented barn and be back out into the real world.

In the second scenario, the one that she knew was the more realistic outcome, Varias Caras would overpower her attempt to snatch the knife and stab her to death. Maybe even worse than that, maybe her resistance would activate some sort of sexual impulses in him and he'd do much worse before killing her.

Just the thought of that was enough to deter her from trying anything too bold. Things were bad, but she was well aware that they could get worse.

He finished undoing all three of the shackles, took her shirt off, cuffed her up again, and then went back to the hose.

"Fresh and clean for Mamá's party," Varias Caras said, turning the faucet on.

Using his thumb, he blocked some of the hose's opening and aimed it at Nadine. The first sprays of water felt like the fingers of a dead person, but after that it got better. Varias Caras sprayed water all over her but made sure not to wet her face.

He didn't want to ruin his makeup job.

Fifteen minutes later, Varias Caras had her dried off, wearing Mamá's red dress, and shackled up again. He stepped back to get a good look at her with a big grin on his face.

Her captor looked her up and down with admiration, but it wasn't with any sexual desire. It was the way a man might look at his favorite sports car after spending an afternoon washing and waxing it.

"*Muy bonita. Me gusta.*" he said, nodding to her. "Mamá's party will be fun. Good time."

"Only…only one other girl, right?" Nadine said, her voice cracking. She wasn't even fully aware that she'd asked the question until it was already coming out of her mouth, but she *had* to know. She had to know that he was only planning on bringing one girl back to suffer with her and not anyone else.

"Yes," Varias Caras said, then dropped his eyes to the floor. With one finger, he reached into the eyehole of his mask and rubbed under his eye. When he brought it back out, Nadine saw it was wet.

My God. He's crying.

"I…I am sorry," he said. "My brain…it cannot handle taking care of two Barbies."

Varias Caras threw himself to the floor, flat on his stomach. His long, curly hair splayed out on the floor looked like a dead crow laying on his head.

"Stupid! Stupid! Stupid!" he yelled out, smashing his fists against the floor.

Nadine felt the floor and the wall behind her vibrate with each one of his strikes, and for a second thought the damn barn was about to collapse and kill them both.

The tantrum only lasted a few seconds, then Varias Caras picked himself up off the floor. He punched himself on the side of the head before saying, "I have to let you go when I bring back other Barbie… I am sorry."

He looked at her. His eyes were wet and shiny behind the grotesque mask.

He's talking to me like I'm a pet he has to put down. Nadine could hardly believe what she was hearing, and the more she thought about it, the more it seemed like that was exactly what was happening. She was a pet to him, nothing more.

No, no. Even less than that. I'm a Barbie. A Barbie doll. The name finally made sense to her after all this time, and her heart quivered in fear.

"I will return later with other Barbie," he continued, "Then tomorrow, after Mamá's party, maybe let you go."

Without waiting for her reply, Varias Caras headed out.

He rolled the barn door shut, staring at her from behind the face that didn't belong to him the entire time. This was one expression Nadine could never figure out, because his eyes were void of any emotion when he was leaving the barn. They were entirely soulless. A pair of dark, dead eyes staring at her from the exit point of her prison.

Tomorrow she might be let go. But there was no promise in his words. There was no promise of a tomorrow for her at all.

CHAPTER 29

Gavin, Fletcher, and Fred were gathered on the front deck, their stomachs filled with breakfast burritos. They were passing a hefty joint around to each other.

The weed was really hitting Fred out here in a way he'd never felt it hit him before. It also didn't help that Gavin had made them all take shots of tequila during breakfast. Either way, the headline of the missing couple article was burning in his mind with an itch he could only scratch by talking about it.

"Hey, did any of you happen to do any digging around about this cabin?"

"What do you mean?" Gavin asked.

"Man, I saw some creepy article about this place," Fred told them.

"What're you talking about?"

"You didn't do much research on Lakewood Cabin, did you?" Fred asked.

"No. Just tell us what you saw—and take a hit and pass it already," Gavin scolded.

Fred grimaced, but took a big hit and reached over the picnic table to hand him the joint. "Saw something about a couple never returning from this place."

"Big whoop," Gavin took a big hit of the joint, and then passed it to Fletcher. "Take a look around us, Fredster. You could get lost looking for a place to take a piss out there."

"No, dude. I think it was something else," Fred argued. "If I had any service out here, I'd pull up the article."

"What else did you find?" Fletcher asked. He felt like the map was burning a hole on the side of his thigh.

"I don't know, that's it. Why?"

"Did you happen to see anything about a campsite?"

"Uh," Fred jogged through his memory. "No?"

"Check this out," Fletcher took the map out of his pocket. "I found it in the game room, behind the entertainment system."

He splayed it out on the picnic table, and Gav and Fred gathered over it. Immediately, they noticed the Sharpie cabins and the name CAMP LAKEWOOD.

"What the hell?" Gavin hooted.

Fred took out the map he had in his pocket and put it on the table next to Fletcher's map. They were indeed maps of the same location, with the obvious difference being the graphics and the added in campgrounds.

"What about this?" Fred asked.

"I don't know. It's just weird that someone drew this stuff on a map and left it behind," Fletcher replied. Now that Fred had posed the question, he wasn't really sure what his point was.

"Must be some abandoned place someone stumbled upon by accident," Fred guessed.

"You guys want to go and try to find this place?" Gavin grinned at them.

"Wh-what if we get lost and don't come back like that couple that disappeared?" Fletcher asked.

Gavin burst out laughing. "Fletch, how fucking high are you?"

"Pretty high."

"Yeah," Gavin continued. "I can tell. Nothing like that is gonna happen to us. We'll just find some campgrounds and that's it. It'll be fun."

Fletcher shook his head and laughed at himself. "Yeah, you're right. Alright, I'm down."

He didn't get much time with the map himself, but this was better anyway. A hike through a forgotten trail sounded like a killer idea.

"What about you, Fred? You in?" Gavin asked.

"Yeah," Fred said, giving in to peer pressure. "Sure, alright. But let's follow the paths on the map. No getting crazy."

"Yeah, yeah, whatever, Fredster." Gavin said, gathering up the maps.

They finished the joint, then went inside the cabin to ask any of the others if they wanted to come.

CHAPTER 30

Emeril drove through the woods, driving faster than he realized. Something pulled him like a magnet, and he knew this first location—"file 3" as Harold Buckley had labeled it in the email—was where his life's work would finally pay off.

He was reminiscing on his years as a psychology graduate student, when his colleagues (and especially the professors) all thought he was insane for his beliefs in the supernatural. Back then, he cared more about what people thought of him, and mostly tried to keep his beliefs to himself. But the whole time, he felt something inside of him that he couldn't ever describe, something that told him there was more to this world than just science and psychology. Things that wouldn't ever be discovered by those who treated the sciences like gospel.

He didn't know what it was then, and didn't know what it was now, but he felt like it would all make sense when they reached the location in file 3's map. When they reached Camp Slaughter...

"Emeril, maybe you should slow down?" Molly suggested.

She noticed the same thing Nadine Lang had noticed more than a year ago driving down a similar road with her husband speeding; if a car was coming in the opposite direction, they'd have a hard time avoiding a head-on collision. It wasn't likely anyone would be driving on this road at the same time, but on the other side of the same coin, totaling a car in such a remote area would make dealing with the aftermath a hassle.

"Sorry," Emeril said, lightening his foot off the pedal. "Just a bit anxious to reach our destination."

"Yeah, I can tell." It came out in a ribbing tone, but she meant it, too.

His face was beaming, almost youthful in appearance. She'd never seen him like this before. It helped to calm her own nerves down—but only to an extent.

"According to the notes Mister Buckley provided us, we should be there in just a little while more." Emeril said, glancing down at the directions splayed out on his lap. "Are you prepared for what we might encounter?"

Molly's mind went to the revolver sitting in the glove compartment. "Yeah, I guess so."

Then she looked out the window and gulped. The trees were endless out there and packed together tightly like an unopened pack of cotton swabs. And the more they drove, the deeper the woods seemed to get. Which meant the more likely it was that anything could be hiding out there.

"We will be fine," Emeril assured her.

"We will be." She said. Then with a weak smile on her face added, "Just make sure you pull your own weight, Emeril."

"I will try to push these old bones as much as possible." Emeril returned the smile.

Those were the last words they said to each other until they reached their destination.

CHAPTER 31

They found the girls in the game room around the ping-pong table. They were holding the paddles and hitting the ball back to each other, but it was more of an activity they were doing between drinking mimosas rather than actually playing. Sound effects from the SNES Wayne and Dalton were playing in a corner of the room filled the air. Over all, the den had the feeling of kids partying bright and early without a care in the world.

Gavin burst through the door. "We're going hiking! Who's coming?"

His announcement stopped the girls' game, and Noelle caught the ball mid-air as they all turned their attention to him.

"What?" Brooke said.

"We're going hiking," Gavin repeated. He unfolded the map Fletcher had found and held it up for them to get a look at it.

The girls looked at one another in confusion as they tried to figure out what was going on.

"Fletcher found this map," Fred started to explain.

"We're gonna loot the fuck out of these cabins," Gavin said proudly, but this just confused the girls more.

Fred ignored him and snatched the map out of his hand. He laid it down flat on the ping-pong table. The girls came around to where he was and crowded around it, peering over his shoulder.

"Someone drew in a campsite that isn't on our map," Fred told them, tracing his finger along the added trail. "We're gonna try to find this path and follow it. See if we find this campsite."

"What if we get lost?" Brooke said.

"We won't. We have the map." Gavin said. "We traveled through these woods out in the dark last night, didn't we?"

"Yeah, I think we'll be fine," Fred said. "And if I'm looking at this map right, we weren't even that far from the campground when we were at the lake last night. If it seems too hard to follow, we'll turn back."

Noelle looked out one of the open windows, and saw the sunrays were still shining down bright through the treetops. She started walking away from the table. "I'll take a raincheck on this one. I'm way too pale to be out in that bright sun."

"Put on some suntan and you're good," Gavin said, but he sensed there was another reason she didn't want to go, and it probably had something to do with her confession to Fred at the lake last night.

She shook her head and looked over at the TV screen where Wayne was trying to guide Mario through Bowser's Castle in *Super Mario Bros. 3* with a series of expletives flying out of his mouth. "I think I'd rather stay back here and chill with them."

"Whatever," Gavin said. "What about you two? Bet you could get some dope pics for your Instagram, Vanessa."

"What if we don't find anything there?" Vanessa said.

"We're still hiking through the beautiful woods. We'll get *something*." After last night's trip, Brooke was excited to explore more of their surroundings, and she really wanted Vanessa to come along with her.

"Yeah, true. Alright, I'm in," Vanessa said.

Fred was blown away by Gavin's persuasive tricks working once again. He really was a natural at it.

"What about you Dalton?" Brooke said to him across the room.

He turned from watching Wayne playing. "I'm sorry, what?"

"You want to come hiking with us?" Brooke repeated the question.

Dalton held the controller up to his cousin and shook his head. "My turn is up next."

"Mister Fun Guy of the Year." Gavin said under his breath. Behind him, he heard Fletcher laugh.

Brooke shot him an icy glare that made them both go silent. "I take it you're leaving Wayne?"

"Why the hell would I want to take him?" Gavin said.

Before their squabble could turn into anything more, Fred started moving. "Enough messing around. Let's go hike off these burritos."

No one protested this, and they all started for their rooms to grab what they needed for the hike.

"You two really brought some buzzkills to this trip," Gavin teased Fred and Brooke.

Fred didn't much feel like defending Noelle. He was still feeling strange about everything that happened, and somewhere in that odd whirlwind of emotions was anger for her. It didn't make sense why she'd even come onto this camping trip with him—or how her boyfriend was OK with it in the first place, until he thought maybe she'd agreed to this trip before their thing got serious and didn't want to bail on him.

At least there's that. He thought sourly.

Brooke turned around, frowning at Gavin. "Dalton's a poet, not an outdoorsman."

"Yeah, well, he could've fooled me with those shirts he wears." Gavin laughed, adding to the insult.

"Oh, shut up, Gav!" Brooke said, scaring some birds out of a tree.

The command seemed to have worked, not just on Gavin, but the rest of the group as they continued down the path in silence. According to the map, they were only a few yards away from the drawn-in trail.

Ten minutes passed.

Fletcher pointed off to the side of the path they were on and said, "Look, guys! I think that's it right there."

They looked. There was a blanket of overgrown wild grass and moss over it, but the path could still be seen if you knew it was there. Underneath the foliage was hardpacked dirt and bits of gravel like what made up the path they were currently on.

"Oh shit, I think it is," Gavin said, walking past the rest of the group. He peered deeper down the path and noticed the unnatural pattern of cleared trees.

"Yeah," Fred said, looking at the map. "This is where the trail is supposed to be according to the map, just off that bend back there."

"Then what're we waiting for?" Gavin asked.

"We're waiting for you to go," Vanessa said.

Gavin snickered, but when he looked back at the hidden path, he felt a sudden unsteadiness. They had no idea what they would find at the end of the trail. And even worse, what if the trail gradually got more hidden as they progressed through it, until eventually it ended, and they didn't know how to get back?

"Come on," Fred said, pushing past him and starting into the trail. "What? Are you afraid?"

Gavin shook his head and trotted after him. "No, Fredster. Definitely not."

CHAPTER 32

IGNACIO APPROACHED THE cabin from the back. Luckily, he knew the woods well enough that he could navigate them without having to follow any set paths. This gave him the advantage of moving through them without being detected and allowed him to surprise his prey, as he was about to do now.

He heard chatter coming from the front of the cabin, so Ignacio headed in that direction. He peered through one of the den windows. Three people were gathered in front of the television.

Two boys and a girl. The girl he recognized. She'd been hiking last night with Mamá's lookalike. That meant they were a part of the same group. Ignacio's brain didn't work right, but that much he could figure out.

Before he made a move, Varias Caras wanted to make sure there wasn't anyone else in the cabin.

Ignacio crouched down and walked alongside the first set of kitchen windows. The counters were riddled with dirty paper plates, tinfoil, plastic utensils, beer cans, liquor bottles, cups, paper towels, and other evidence of partying, but there was no one there.

Ignacio moved on to the next window, which was an opaque one that belonged to the first floor bathroom. He put his ear (well, the ear of the person whose face he was wearing) up to it. If there was someone inside, they'd likely notice his shadow, and start screaming. He listened for the scream.

Nothing. Not even the sounds of someone peeing or pooing or washing their hands.

Sure that the bathroom was unoccupied, he moved onto the next room. A small study room with books crammed in shelves and a single Lazy-Boy. Also empty.

Ignacio continued to move alongside the perimeter of the cabin, peering into the rooms. He knew the cabin's layout very well; he'd been here many times. He realized the further away he got from the game room, the stiller the cabin grew.

Positive there wasn't anyone else in the cabin, he made his way back around to the den to take another peek.

They still didn't notice him. They were too focused on the TV screen.

Ignacio counted them with an index finger to make sure they were all still there.

One. Two. Three.

Yep, all there.

None of them were the Mamá lookalike, but that was OK. The Mamá lookalike and the others must have gone out into the woods. That was what campers did when they came out here. Explore.

Ignacio would return later to capture her and bring her to the barn.

For now, though, his mind turned to the youngest kid in the group. He was younger than the people he usually ran into out here, which meant his meat would be more tender. It would probably fall right off the bone.

Ignacio's stomach grumbled.

He pulled the machete from the sheath on his back.

Wayne was on the last level of *Super Mario Bros. 3*. The Bill the Bullets were flying across the screen, trying to take him out of the game. Lakitu was throwing spiked shells from his cloud in the sky, covering the stage with hazards Wayne had to guide Mario safely away from.

He was down to his last life, and a few wrong moves meant the dreaded GAME OVER screen.

His skin was getting clammy, but the controller may as well have been glued in his hands. Wayne was in the zone.

But the zone was about to be shattered.

As he'd expected, the front cabin door was unlocked. It always was. It didn't make much sense to Varias Caras, but campers felt safe out here—despite that they were invading the spots of large predatory animals.

It was almost as if they feared their own species more than the wild ones.

And maybe that made sense, considering what he was about to do to them.

Sound effects and video game music filled the otherwise still cabin. Mario jumping, collecting coins, getting power-ups, sounds that reminded Ignacio of childhood.

For a moment, he wanted to go in there and play with them.

We're not here to play, idiota. We're here to hunt, Varias Caras said to him.

"*Si, si…*" Ignacio responded aloud, disappointed.

He made the innocent part of his mind—the part that was the most Ignacio—go back into its hidey hole.

The cabin was built out of such sturdy wood that there was no creaking even underneath his heavy boots. A godsend for someone that enjoyed the element of surprise.

He stood out in the hallway, but all three of them were watching the television screen and just as they didn't notice him at the window, they didn't notice him approaching here, either.

Varias Caras readied the machete.

It was killing time.

Dalton saw him out of the corner of his eye first. A gigantic man rushed toward them. He wanted to scream, but he couldn't do anything, his brain was too scrambled by fear to send the proper signals to the rest of his body.

The only thing he could move were his eyes, and they dropped down to the object the man held in his left hand. It was a machete. Dalton brought his eyes back up to the man's face, to see if maybe he didn't have any bad intentions. Maybe he was just a yard worker coming to let them know he was here, and he was being a "pussy" as his older brothers called him for writing poetry—then his eyes landed on the man's face.

There was no expression on it. And even more confusing, it looked stiff as bark.

Time seemed to speed up suddenly.

Dalton looked back down at the machete in time to see the man's massive knuckles tightening around the handle. His instincts had been right. This was no yard worker at all.

The scream finally came out of him, alerting the others.

Perhaps too late, but better than never.

CHAPTER 33

At the end of their hike, they found the abandoned campsite. The cabins were rundown, looking like they were one stiff breeze away from toppling over. The yards were all overgrown, in some spots it was brown and wispy, in others it was thick and green with plenty of weeds growing out of it.

Vines of morning glory grew on the side of the rotting cabins, adding some colorfulness to the otherwise drab scenery. Some of the vines had found holes in the broken windows and continued to grow inside along the floors and walls. The sight was something to behold; the in between stages of man's abandoned constructions being swallowed up by the beauty of nature.

Gavin walked up the porch steps of the nearest cabin. They creaked underneath him, threatening to break under his weight, but they held strong. The floorboards on the porch didn't feel any less rickety as he walked across them, either. He stopped in front of one of the windows and blew dust off it, then looked inside.

He was looking at a front office. A desk sat in the middle of the room, with sticky notes, computer paper, and pens littered on it. Behind the desk there was an office chair with a broken headrest that slanted to the right like the head of a man slumbering on a train. In a corner a bookshelf crammed with trophies, photos of camping groups, and binders sat behind a film of spiderweb. Forgotten paintings of forests and mountains (*Stupid.* Gavin thought. *Why would you put nature inside when it was just outside the window?*) decorated the walls of the office and the walls of the corridors he could see.

The place somehow looked abandoned and busy at the same time, almost like the people one day just disappeared in the middle of a work day. More than likely, this was just junk they didn't care about, and no one removed, but it made Gavin feel like someone was about to come around the corner at any moment and shoo them away.

"Yo, check this out!" Fred called to him.

Gavin turned away from the cabin, giving it a wary sideways glance before going to join the others. Fred and the girls were standing in front of a sign at the front of the office he'd walked right past.

The sign was a six-by-six wooden board that was large enough to greet visitors from a distance. Time and weather had taken its toll on the wood, and pieces of the sign were scattered on the grass island it stood on. There were scratch marks on the top of it where birds had latched their claws on while they basked in the sun and preened themselves.

A fading family of three was painted on the sign. Their faces and the canoe they rode on were nothing but blurs now. Yellow and blue paint that used to make up the sun and sky behind the family were now just random blotches of color scattered around them. Maybe at some point this had been a happy scene, but time had worn that away as much as the wood it was on.

Above the family were the words WELCOME TO CAMP LAKEWOOD in a color that once had been golden, but now was a dark brown that blended in with the wood and was almost illegible. Someone had taken care of that, though, and spray painted the word SLAUGHTER in bright red over LAKEWOOD, so that the sign read:

WELCOME TO CAMP SLAUGHTER

"Camp Slaughter," Fletcher laughed. "Isn't that the title of a *Goosebumps* book?"

"That was *Ghost Camp*," Fred corrected him.

"Oh, yeah. Right," Fletcher said.

"This is a little more…uh, morbid, wouldn't you say?" Fred said.

"I wonder who did this…and why they were carrying red spray paint in the first place," Brooke chimed in.

"Hey," Gavin said, "do any of you have cellphone service out here?"

Fred turned to him, shaking his head. "What the hell kind of question is that? We haven't had cellphone service since we were halfway to the cabin yesterday."

"Yeah," Gavin said, taking a look at the abandoned camp that surrounded them. He hadn't been able to kick off the funk peering into the cabin had put him into. "I know, I was just wondering. I guess the people who camped here didn't have cellphone service, either."

"Probably not," Fred said, taking a closer look at his face. "You alright, man?"

"Yeah, yeah," Gavin said, shrugging. "What? You think I'm scared?"

Fred laughed it off, but he thought maybe that was the truth considering he brought it up first. "No, man. Definitely not you."

Gavin ignored his sarcasm, and to the group said, "We just gonna stand here, or are we gonna look around?"

"Yeah, let's see what else we find," Fletcher said.

"This place is creeping me out," Vanessa said.

Gavin, afraid that the others knew he was creeped out too, started to overcompensate his bravery. "It's just a bunch of old cabins. There's nothing to worry about—if anything does happen, I'll protect you."

There was a nervous tremble of laughter in the group as they followed him into the campgrounds.

They had no way of knowing this, but it was what was going to find them that they should have worried about.

CHAPTER 34

It was Noelle who jumped into gear first. She slammed the game room door shut on the hallway before the man could reach them, and threw the lock. "Out the windows!" she shouted at the boys.

Dalton and Wayne had been frozen in terror, with looks on their faces like they'd just shit their pants, but the command shook them out of it. They sprang into action, running to the window closest to them.

Dalton was fidgeting with the screen window when a thought occurred to him. "Wait! Wait! What if there are others outside?"

"Shit," Noelle stopped mid climb out of the window and sat down on the ledge. She swung her legs back inside the cabin. *He's right.*

But there was no time to think.

The intruder kicked at the door, as if to put an exclamation point on the thought.

BANG. BANG. BANG.

The kicks were strong, but the door was holding…for now.

"Put something in front of the door!" Noelle said to Dalton.

Dalton understood the change of strategy and ran over to the entertainment system where the SNES was setup. He grabbed it and dragged it across the floor as hard as he could, finished and polished wood be damned. The TV went crashing off the back as the cord caught at the end of its length. The gaming system went with it. With one final sad electronic glurp, Mario faded to black.

Wayne jumped back into the cabin and ran over to the other side of the furniture to help speed up the process. The entertainment system's legs screeched as they sliced streaks into the wooden floor.

Meanwhile, Noelle was working on closing the windows, aware that the place would quickly turn into a sweatbox without any air conditioning.

Better sweating than dead, she thought.

Now that they had the furniture in place and (it seemed, for the time being, anyhow) that the added weight was successfully holding their intruder at bay, Dalton and Wayne each went to a set of windows to close and lock them. If there were more intruders out there, they could easily break the glass, but they'd at least be alerted of where they were coming from.

With the windows secured, they gathered in the center of the room by the pool table, away from any windows in case glass did start flying through the air.

Wayne threw his arms around Noelle. He didn't mean it in any perverted way, it was more a gesture of him searching for comfort. He buried his head into her shoulder and cried. "I want my mom."

Holding onto each other, they both crumpled to the ground. Noelle ran her fingers through his hair and put her head on top of his.

"Wayne, stop. We'll be okay. We will," she whispered to him, but she didn't believe it herself.

Didn't believe it at all. And she started to cry, too.

CHAPTER 35

"THERE IT IS!" Emeril called out.

They were greeted by the same sign Gavin and company had just been looking at a few minutes ago. Both Emeril and Molly read the sign with the graffitist's fix:

WELCOME TO CAMP SLAUGHTER

Emeril could hardly believe his eyes. It was exactly the name Harold Buckley had used. He swallowed. "Molly, grab your camera!"

"On it, Emeril," she said, reaching into the backseat. She powered the camera on, hit record, and pointed it at the sign. "What're you thinking, Emeril?"

"I'm thinking, I've never been to Disneyland—but if I had gone as a child, this is probably how I would have felt," he said.

The Subaru came around the last curve before the road straightened out and went up the hill to the campgrounds. Molly looked over her shoulder and saw Emeril's face was flushed red and his eyes were shiny. The stoic man was barely visible in this jubilant face. It was the most excited she'd ever seen him, and all they'd seen so far was a sign.

"The grove is supposed to be somewhere around here," Emeril said.

"And in the grove, the cannibal's hideout?" Molly said. "Am I remembering that right?"

"Yes, yes. Precisely," Emeril said.

He clutched the steering wheel tighter as he felt that tremble in his organs again. This time, though, he was ready for it, and kept control of himself. He felt his insides moving; his heart, his lungs, his bones, his blood, his arteries, even the fillings in his teeth, it all moved like people in a stadium doing the wave. Except, nothing was physically moving. This was nothing more than a feeling, a feeling that something supernatural was near.

Emeril was sure that's what this new sensation was. It was a sign that he was on the path of his destiny. He'd stayed up all last night, looking at the cracks in the ceiling of the shoddy cabin, wondering if he was losing his mind or not, but now he was sure he wasn't.

They were going to uncover something huge.

Emeril Dantes didn't know this, because he could only feel the energy emitting from the campsite—or rather, the energy emitting from the space the campsite was built on—but they were heading to a part of the Earth where spirit energy was collected. A space where the living and the dead world touched each other. It was only a soft touch, a gentle kiss between the two worlds, where only those born with an extra sense could ever feel the interaction. It was a place where lost spirits roamed, waiting for their day to finally cross over into the next realm for good.

Emeril and Molly were headed into haunted lands, to put it in simple terms.

CHAPTER 36

IGNACIO KICKED THE door two more times, but it wouldn't budge. Whatever they'd put in front of it was too heavy to knock over.

He had to get them another way. The machete could hack through the door and make a hole big enough for him to squeeze through, but that would take forever. They'd escape out of the room through the windows by the time the hole was big enough.

The windows. Yes. He could use the windows to get inside.

He made his way out of the cabin and went around to that side of the cabin. He saw his prey huddled in the center of the room inside. What he could see of their faces was as pale as horchata.

Using the handle of the machete, he smashed a window. The exploding glass got their attention.

The girl made a sound that was a cross between a scream and a sob. The cry of fear.

Ignacio smiled.

The blue-haired guy got up and started for a part of the room Ignacio couldn't see. It didn't matter, he was going to kill them all.

He switched the machete into his other hand and reached inside the window to unlock it. Then, with the same hand, he threw it open.

Before he could start to climb inside to begin killing, the blue-haired guy returned, and Ignacio realized the trio wasn't as helpless as he thought.

Stupid Ignacio…

Dalton heard the glass shatter, and knew it was time for him to act. A fourteen-year-old kid and a petite girl weren't going to be the ones to get them out of this bind, so it was all on his shoulders.

As absurd as it was, he heard his brothers laughing at that thought in his mind.

Ignoring the laughter, he ran over to the bucket of darts, scooped some up in his hand, and then ran back to the center of the room. The giant man was in the middle of climbing into the window. Without bothering to take aim, Dalton threw a dart in his direction.

By some great stroke of luck, the dart went into Varias Caras' face, into the side of his mouth where the mask didn't cover. It pierced through his cheek, stopping just short of his tongue.

Ignacio screamed, and fell backward out of the window, spitting blood into the air. He picked himself up to his knees, pulled the dart from his cheek, and threw it over his shoulder. Trying to ignore the pain in his face, he started back through the window.

Dalton launched another dart. Somehow, his shaking hands still had true aim. The dart went into Ignacio's brow, right into the exposed part of his face above the right eye. Blood oozed down into it. He didn't fall back this time, instead, he threw himself through the window like a man on fire diving into water.

Out of pure reflex, Dalton threw another dart, but his luck had run out. The dart missed entirely, whizzed past Varias Caras, and went out the window.

Ignacio got up to his feet and ripped the dart out of his face. Then he swung the machete through the air in a blind rage.

Dalton hopped back, but he was too slow.

The machete went through his neck, cutting it open on a diagonal. His head snapped back, tendons in his neck stretched to their limits like the roots of a stump being pulled from the earth. His head remained attached to his body only by the neckbone and some scraps of skin.

Ignacio pulled on the handle of the machete, and since it was still stuck in Dalton, he pulled the kid toward him. At the same time, he punched him in the jaw. The impact was enough to break the neck bone, and the last bits of skin ripped as Dalton's head went flying off his shoulders.

The head tumbled through the air, struck one of the walls with a wet splat, and then fell to the ground. It bounced on the floor a few times before coming to a rolling stop. Dalton's face stared up at the spinning ceiling fan with an agonized expression.

Ignacio stomped on the lifeless corpse for leverage and pulled the machete out of it. Then he readied it for the next kill.

While this was happening, the girl had climbed out of the cabin and was running into the woods. But it didn't matter right now. He only cared about the young kid.

The fresh meat.

Wayne was halfway out of the window when Ignacio grabbed him by the belt loops of his pants. He yanked on him, but Wayne clung on the sill with both hands.

This was nothing new to Ignacio. They always did this. But he was stronger than them…always stronger.

Ignacio pulled harder. Wayne lost his grip and fell to the floor hard enough to break one of his ribs. He screamed, but the scream got caught in his throat as Ignacio stomped on his back and knocked the breath out of him. His ribs crunched some more underneath the pressure of the big boot.

Wayne tried squirming away from him, but it was no use, the guy was too big and strong. It felt like an anvil had fallen on him. Wayne kicked and punched the air and started to cry, but he knew this was as pointless as the squirming.

Ignacio drove the tip of the machete through the back of the kid's neck, all the way through until it was stuck in the wooden floor. Wayne's limbs continued to thrash through the air, but it was nothing but his muscles spasming as he died. After a few seconds, his whole body went still.

Blood from the wound began to run down and pool around the boy's head, sopping his hair and turning it red. It didn't matter, Ignacio didn't like the head anyway. That was the part of his prey he always threw in the trash after peeling the skin for his masks.

Ignacio peered out of the windows to see where the girl was. He could still see her sprinting in the trees—or at least going at a pace that was her version of sprinting. She was slow. He could catch her if he hurried, maybe…

But no. The important one was Mamá's lookalike, who wasn't here. Which meant he'd have to go looking for her later. For now, though, he was done here.

Ignacio returned to the young kid. He pulled the machete out of his neck, then chopped his head off. No point in keeping it attached.

With one hand, he lifted the boy up and put him on his shoulder.

He started out of the den, glancing over at the headless body that used to belong to the blue-haired kid in the middle of the room. He'd have to leave it behind, unfortunately. Ignacio didn't like leaving corpses behind.

That was one thing Mamá had drilled into him. Don't play with your food and don't waste any.

Hay gente que no tienen de comer.

There are people who don't have anything to eat.

And here he was, walking away leaving behind a perfectly full human body that would have fed him for weeks.

It didn't feel good to waste food. Didn't feel good at all.

CHAPTER 37

"WHAT IS THAT?" Molly said, looking around the camera and pointing to what appeared to be people moving between the cabins in the distance.

"Hikers," Emeril said, throwing her a sideways glance. "Did you think it was spirits?"

Molly laughed. "No, screw you Emeril. Just taken by surprise. Nobody's supposed to know where this place is."

"Right. So. Shall we find out what they're doing here?" It was more of a statement than a question considering he was unfastening his seatbelt as he spoke.

They were parked in front of the CAMP SLAUGHTER sign, and a quick glance at the cabins that made up the place confirmed that this was indeed the spot Harold Buckley had told them about. Emeril had sobered up from the high of finding the place, and though he no longer felt the wave of energy going through him, he still had the sense that there was something supernatural here.

"Yeah, let's go talk to them," Molly said. Then she started reaching for the glove compartment where they kept the revolver.

"No need for that," Emeril said, lifting his shirt up to reveal the pistol holstered to his hip. "This should be enough. You bring that with you."

He was referring to the camera.

"And if they're dangerous, you think I'll be able to record them to death?" Molly retorted.

"I don't think it's necessary we stroll up to them strapped like cowboys," Emeril said. "Please, Molly? We need to capture this… all of this…"

"Alright," Molly said, seeing his face weakening. "Okay, fine. But I better not regret this."

"I'll do all of the talking. You just stay back and record. It will be fine. I promise."

Molly didn't respond, just climbed out of the car. On the driver's side, Emeril did the same.

Like the first cabin Gavin had peered into, the campgrounds looked like they'd been abandoned in the middle of a busy day. Targets in the archery range still had arrows sticking out of their grimy, faded faces. There was a small lake near the campground with a lonesome, filthy canoe sitting on its bank.

Gavin and Fletcher went up to one of the lodging cabins, which were much smaller than the office cabin, and peered inside it. Most of the space inside was taken up by a bunkbed that had collapsed on itself. A mess of splinters stuck out from the support columns where they'd broken. Seeds and spores had found cracks in the floor and grown into wildflowers and fungi. By the looks of it, this was the only life the cabin had seen in years.

"Want to go inside?" Gavin said.

Fletcher looked away from his window and over at Gavin to see if he was serious. "For what?"

"I don't know…" Gavin shrugged. "Just to see what else we find."

Fred was coming up the porch steps to join them and heard Gavin's suggestion. "Man, you always have to be messing around, huh?"

"What?" Gavin whirled around to face him. "Come on, Fredster, it's not like we're going to get into trouble."

"Let's just leave it alone," Fred said.

"I don't get it, why?"

Fred shrugged. "I don't know. It just feels...wrong to disturb things around here."

Gavin knew what he meant, which was the reason *why* he wanted to do it. The only way he'd ever known how to deal with uncomfortable feelings was by confronting whatever was making him feel that way. And right now, these stupid campgrounds were doing it to him. He'd feel better kicking down one of these cabin doors.

"Just leave it alone," Fred repeated. "Let's just go take pictures with the girls over there."

The girls were out front of another cabin, taking selfies for Vanessa's Instagram. Despite their initial resistance, they seemed to be having a good time—a better time than even the guys—and were laughing and joking as they looked over the pictures on their phones.

"Now who's acting scared, Fredster?" Gavin smirked.

But just as quickly as the smirk came it disappeared. His lips went flat as he saw a light in the distance. Because of the strange mood the place had him in, he thought it was something supernatural for a second.

But no. It wasn't anything supernatural. Just as surprising, though perhaps not as frightful, it was a pair of headlights. The lights went off, and all Gavin was looking at now was the front of an old car parked outside the campgrounds.

"What the hell?" Gavin said. The car seemed to have come out of nowhere. In their distraction, none of them had even heard it coming. This was strange.

Fred and Fletcher turned around to see what had his attention in time to see the Subaru.

"Whoa. Who is that?" Fred said.

"How should I know?" Gavin snapped.

"Should we get out of here?"

Gavin's response was to climb down the cabin porch steps and walk over to the girls, who as of yet hadn't noticed the unexpected visitors.

"Hey, girls, sorry to cut your photoshoot short—but we got company," he said, approaching Vanessa and Brooke.

The girls put their phones down and looked at Gavin's face to see if he was serious. They saw the other boys coming toward them behind Gavin, with similarly long expressions.

"What? What're you talking about?" Brooke said.

"Look," Gavin pointed behind them.

They spun around, and nearly jumped out of their shoes when they saw the vehicle.

"Oh shit!" Vanessa said, hopping backward. "Are they park rangers?"

The car doors opened, and they saw an older man wearing a chauffeur hat and a Hawaiian shirt getting out of the driver's side. From the passenger side a thin blond woman got out. The object around her neck flashed underneath the sunlight. If Gavin hadn't seen the headlights first, the way this object shined would've made him think about ghosts.

"No way they're park rangers," Gavin said, getting a second look at their visitors. "Not dressed like that."

The others agreed. The old man looked like he'd just gotten off the plane from his first trip to Thailand, rather than someone dressed to deal with trouble in the woods. But that realization only made this all more confusing.

"We should get the fuck out of here," Vanessa said, chewing on the nail of her index finger.

"No," Gavin said, stepping in front of the group. "We have as much right to be here as they do."

"Gav, what're you doing?" Fred asked. "This is no time to be stubborn."

"Shut up, Fredster."

Gavin took a few more steps toward the pair of strangers.

Less than twenty yards separated the two groups now. Gavin puffed his chest out some, and then yelled out, "Hey! Who are you?"

To his surprise, and the surprise of the others, the old man stopped in his tracks.

Emeril sensed the fear coming from the boy—the one he was thinking of as the "leader" of the group. He could almost feel the fear in the air, and he thought of the wave that had vibrated through his body. Surely, that had something to do with his suddenly heightened perception. And more than that, there was no doubt in his mind, this camp was the cause of it.

They were standing on grounds that had inexplicable powers. Or perhaps, grounds that awoke latent abilities in people. Emeril wasn't sure which one it was, but that was something he would ponder later. Right now, he had to figure out who these campers were and what they were doing here.

The leader shouted a question aggressively at them, and Emeril stopped with about twenty yards between them. The group looked like nothing more than some young adults hiking on a summer day, but with how much fear was exuding from them, he was worried they might go into attack mode at the drop of a hat.

Better to approach them with caution.

"Not quite the ghosts we were expecting," Molly said.

Emeril looked over at her. Her face—and the energy he could feel coming from her—suggested she was the same old Molly as she always was. She wasn't experiencing anything close to what he was, which supported his second theory that these grounds were awakening something in him rather than creating them.

"No," Emeril said, "but even the least ferocious animal can be dangerous when threatened."

"Hey assholes! Did you hear me?" the leader shouted at them. At some point when they'd been talking to each other, the boy had picked up a long stick from the ground. He held it in his hands like it was a sword.

"Please, young man. There is no need for such language and hostility," Emeril said, taking a few steps closer.

"Hey! Don't move until you tell us who you are."

"Sure, sure," Emeril said. "My name is Emeril Dantes. The young lady behind me is Molly Sanger. We're filmmakers out here doing a documentary on this abandoned campground."

"Filmmakers?" It was Fred who asked the question.

Gavin grimaced at him.

Seeing the boy relaxing his posture, Emeril dared to get a little closer. "Yes, yes. As you can see, my partner has a camera with her. I assure you, we come in peace."

He smiled at them, and now he felt the group dynamic change. The emotion in the air went from fear and anxiety to interest and curiosity. Except for the leader, who still seemed riled up.

"If you don't mind," Emeril said to them, "We would like to get closer to the camp. Perhaps at a closer distance, we can have a clearer conversation and I can better explain what we're doing out here."

"I wish somebody would explain all this," Vanessa blurted out.

Gavin turned to her and shot her a dirty look that she ignored. There was a murmur of agreement between the group and then, to the chagrin of the leader, they were inviting Emeril and Molly to come join them at the camp.

"Well done," Molly said.

"Sometimes it just takes the right words to get the job done," Emeril said, as they started up to meet with the group.

"What're you guys doing?" Gavin hissed. He was pissed off at all of them, but especially Fred and Vanessa for being at the forefront of the invitation. "You guys have no idea who these creepos are."

"Chill out," Fred told him. "That guy looks as threatening as my grandpa and that woman looks like a spin class instructor."

Gavin pushed past them. "I'm getting out of here. If it turns out those two ask you to be in some weird ass outdoor porn movie, don't say I didn't warn you."

"No need to fret, young man," Emeril said. He was standing at a comfortable conversation distance from the group now. "Of course, you're free to leave if you have no interest."

"Damn right I'm free to leave," Gavin said, laughing. "I didn't need your permission, old man. Sayonara."

He marched toward the path they'd hiked to get here.

"Wait, Gav!" Brooke called after him, but it was no use, he kept on going ahead as if he hadn't heard her. To the others, Brooke said, "I'm gonna go with him—Maybe I'll be able to convince him to come back."

"Don't bother," Fred said, knowing how stubborn Gavin was.

"He doesn't have the map, though. What if he gets lost?"

"Oh well," Fred said. "That's on him. He's a big boy."

"Jeez, that's a bit harsh, don't you think?"

"Yeah, man," Fletcher agreed. "Maybe we should go get him."

Fred clenched his hands into fists. Up until now, he hadn't been looking at anyone directly in the face, but now he turned to look at Brooke and Fletcher. There was a rage inside of him that had been building up that he wasn't aware of until now.

Anger at being rejected by Noelle, anger at Gavin for being a big baby, anger at the others for wanting to bend to Gavin's whim, anger that he wasn't sure he'd land a job after college and he might be working at that computer shop the rest of his life, anger at the uncertainty of his future.

But there was one more underlying factor to his anger, something he couldn't pinpoint. Fred Meyers didn't know this, but it was the power of these campgrounds—of Camp Slaughter—channeling through his body and twisting his emotions into a bottleneck that was about to pop.

"Fuck him!" Fred yelled. Then he cupped his hands around his mouth, and to Gavin he yelled out, "You hear me? Fuck you, you pussy!"

Gavin half-turned around but didn't say anything. Instead, he just turned back around, glad that he was too far for them to see the hurt look on his face.

The others were stunned into silence.

CHAPTER 38

While the group had been splitting up and quibbling, Emeril had wandered into the campgrounds.

They'd done it. They'd found Camp Slaughter. They were going to be the ones to put the kibosh on the debates of its existence, but as he looked around, he wondered at what cost.

Dominating it all, because it was the biggest building, was a large wooden cabin labeled DINING HALL. The other structures were scattered around the dining hall, the angle of their placement making a rough circle. Behind him, the way they'd come in from, was the camp office. It sat several yards away from the core campgrounds.

Behind the lodging cabins on the east side of the campgrounds, there was a broken and ruined playground. Steps were missing in the rope ladder leading up to a rusty slide, some of the jungle gym platforms had holes in them, the monkey bars were rusted, the swing set was missing all of its seats so that the only thing that remained were chains hanging from a bar. What once would have been a playset for children now looked like a collection of deathtraps and torture devices.

And really, the playground told the story of the camp as a whole. There was no joy left in the place, even in the spots made pretty by nature's touch. Anything that may have been painted colorfully was now faded. The wood on the cabins was spotted dark and swelled like skin suffering from leprosy. In some instances, the wood was so bloated it'd burst open and begun to splinter.

With no electricity in them, the insides of the cabins were dark. It didn't matter that it was summer, and the sun was out in full force. There were corners inside, far away from windows, that hadn't seen an ounce of light in years.

No longer were the cabins filled with laughter and chatter from campers. The grassy hills, now covered rampantly by weeds, would never be rolled down or played on by children. At nights, families wouldn't be gathered around the firepits roasting hotdogs and melting smores.

There was no life left in the place.

Camp Slaughter. A fitting name indeed, Emeril thought, drawing in a deep breath.

In the coming minutes, though, the name would make even more sense.

CHAPTER 39

NOELLE WAS LYING flat on top of a boulder. She had no idea where she was. She'd heard the screams from inside the cabin as she'd climbed out the window and bolted into the woods and ran as fast as she could with no idea of her direction.

At the time, it seemed like her only option. If there were others with the machete man, her only chance at survival would have been to outrun them, so she'd ran until it felt like her lungs were going to explode and her knees were going to break. She'd finally stopped in the middle of a small clearing of trees with a giant boulder in the center. She climbed on top of it for no reason other than to avoid being bitten by a snake or a rodent.

Now, she was listening for any signs of someone approaching. But there was nothing. Only her heartbeat slowing down with each breath she took.

In the distance, nuts and fruits clattered against tree branches as they fell from trees, chipmunks scurried through the shrubbery, and a woodpecker's knocks echoed through the woods. But other than that, there was nothing alarming happening around her.

Noelle let out a deep sigh, but at the end of it there wasn't relief the way she thought there would be. Instead, a wave of guilt filled her.

She left Dalton and Wayne behind. Even after she'd told Wayne they'd be OK… Now he was probably dead—correction—*they* were probably dead.

She'd ran and left them behind, left them there to die.

Just like she'd done to her little sister, Rachel.

Noelle buried her head in her arms and wept.

CHAPTER 40

"Your movies go on YouTube?" Vanessa asked the filmmaker duo excitedly.

"Yeah," Molly said, but she was distracted by the same thing that had Emeril's attention.

Emeril was at the edge of the campgrounds, staring out into the distance. About half a mile away from them was a grove of trees. The trees were packed together tightly, and the treetops crossed each other in a way that almost made it look like they were creating a giant thatched roof. In the middle of this grove, there was a shoddy farmhouse. If she took a picture of where they stood from this house, something told her the distance would be the same as in the ear necklace picture Harold Buckley had showed them. And if *that* were true, that meant…

Molly gulped.

"How many subscribers do you guys have?" Vanessa asked.

Since Emeril explained to them what they were doing out here in Camp Slaughter, the Instagram girl was peppering them with nonstop questions about the YouTube channel and kept reminding them how much it sucked that there wasn't any service out here to check it out. The others seemed enthused, but their excitement was dwarfed in comparison.

"Around a hundred thousand or so," Molly said. She walked up next to Emeril, away from the group before another question was flung at her.

"Are you thinking what I'm thinking?" she said to him.

"Mm-hmm, I believe so," Emeril said. "Before we go there, I want to see what's inside that barn."

Until he pointed at it, Molly had somehow missed the big barn on a field between where they stood and the farmhouse. The barn looked to have been built in the same fashion as the other structures on the campgrounds and was just as weathered and worn. Except for the door, which looked new, and stuck out even from this distance.

"There's something going on here," Emeril said. He meant two things at once but wasn't going to bring up the supernatural feelings to Molly, not unless she did so first. What he was referring to was that all the evidence was adding up to human activity in the vicinity.

"Yeah," Molly concurred. "Maybe our friend Harold turned out not to be such a kook after all, huh?"

"Get the camera ready," Emeril said, and they both started toward the barn.

"Hey, I thought you guys were going to interview us?" Brooke called out to them.

Without turning around, Emeril shot his hand out in the air in a quick, dismissive wave.

"After our preliminary investigation, youngsters."

The group all looked at one another, unsure of what to do now.

"Should we go with them?" Fred suggested.

"Why not?" Fletcher said. "It's not like there's much to look at here."

The rest of them showed their agreement with this decision by following behind the two filmmakers.

CHAPTER 41

Now that he was getting closer to the campgrounds, Ignacio's super hearing picked up on the chatter somewhere in the woods. Human voices had a funny way of traveling, they bounced off tree trunks and echoed in a way that made them sound like they were coming from every direction. It was confusing to find where they were coming from sometimes.

Worse than that, Varias Caras was nowhere to be found. That part of his brain had gone to sleep, after the killings back at the cabin.

"Wakey, wakey... Please?" Ignacio pleaded with the monster inside of him, but it was no use. Ignacio was on his own for now, so he continued walking through the woods.

He was following the shortcut from the cabin back to the campgrounds, and the closer he got home, the easier it was to zero in on where the voices were coming from. He walked in that direction, stepping as lightly as he could.

Oh, no, no, no, no, Ignacio thought as he spotted the group walking across the field toward the barn.

They were going to find his Barbie.

This is not good. Not Good. Not Good! Varias Caras, I need help…please help, please!

But there was no reply. Varias Caras was still slumbering.

Ignacio crouched behind the bushes. He dropped the kid from his shoulder, there was a heavy thud as the dead weight crashed to the ground. Ignacio pulled the mask off his face, then put it back on several times, hoping that in some way this would wake Varias Caras.

It didn't.

This whole mess was up to him to fix.

He looked over at where the people were. There was no doubt they were going to inspect the barn. And each second he wasted, they got closer and closer to it. He had to act.

There was less than a quarter mile of trees between him and the field where the group were walking, if he was quiet, he would catch them by surprise.

Yes. That would certainly make things easier. But that didn't mean it was going to be easy.

Ignacio unsheathed the machete from his back, then started toward them.

CHAPTER 42

"This isn't the big sister I remember," Rachel's voice stirred Noelle out of wallowing in her own pity.

She lifted her head up, and saw her little sister standing underneath a shaded area in the woods. The right side of her face was shiny—from blood, no doubt, even though she couldn't make out the color because of the shadows the trees cast over Rachel's face.

"Rach, what're you doing out here?" She wiped the tears from her eyes. The tears were cold.

How long had she been sitting here, wasting time feeling sorry for herself? She wasn't sure, but she knew it was too long.

"Don't you know by now that I'm always with you, Noelle?" Rachel laughed.

"Oh yeah," Noelle said. The truth was, in the panic of everything that'd happened to her, she wasn't sure of anything. "You're not…you're not real."

"I guess that depends, doesn't it?"

Noelle sat up on the rock and shook her head. It was just like her little sister to talk in confusing riddles. "What're you talking about?"

"I'm a manifestation of your anxiety and guilt—and those two things are real, aren't they?" Rachel stepped out into the light, letting Noelle get a better look at her.

Rachel's right eye was out of its socket, dangling down like a paddleball. The entire right side of her body was covered in lacerations oozing with blood. The white sock sticking above her Chuck Taylor's was drenched red.

"You left them behind, just like you did to me, Noelle," Rachel said, grinning.

Noelle clenched her fists. "Stop it. Stop!"

"This is your second chance." Rachel started pacing back and forth, every few steps hiding her back in the shadows, but no matter the lighting, Noelle could see her perfectly white teeth in her grinning mouth.

"What're you going to do, Noelle? Run away and let them die? Like you did to me?"

"Stop!" Noelle covered her ears and buried her head between her knees. "I—I didn't mean to. I didn't mean to leave you there."

"But you did, big sister. That's all that matters. All that matters is what you did, not what you meant."

"Stop!" Noelle opened her eyes, for the first time ever, hoping her sister was gone.

To her surprise, the hallucination *had* vanished. It was just her in the woods again. She took in a deep breath and sighed.

But as she did that, she saw a shadow crawl its way over her. Noelle turned and saw her little sister wasn't gone at all. No, in fact, she was closer than ever. Rachel was sitting on the boulder next to her, her legs dangling off the edge and facing away from her. Noelle saw there were splatters of blood on the back of Rachel's head and tank top.

"Do you remember the summer when we stayed up way past our bedtime and you would read Shakespeare to me?" Rachel asked her.

She remembered that summer very well, and she wanted to say so, but she couldn't. The nostalgic feelings, the sad nostalgic feelings, the question brought with it had her tripped up. Her tongue felt too heavy to move, and an eruption of fresh tears threatened to come out of her.

"Cowards die many times before their deaths; the valiant never taste of death but once." Rachel looked over her shoulder. Her long, auburn hair was covering the damaged side of her face, while the good side was in plain sight, grinning at Noelle. "That was my favorite part. Go back to the cabin, big sister. Be valiant. I know you can be."

Before Noelle could respond, her little sister disappeared into thin-air.

Noelle waited a few seconds, to see if the hallucination was gone for good. When she was sure it was, she slid off the boulder and scanned the area she was in. Trees as far as the eye could see. She thought this must be how someone lost at sea felt, trapped in a seemingly directionless expanse.

"I have no idea where I'm going, Rach," Noelle was whispering, like she always did when her sister visited her. She didn't want others to think she talked to herself—although she was aware that was exactly what she was doing when talking to her hallucinations.

Just pick a direction and go, she told herself. *What's the worst that can happen?*

Noelle started walking, moving steadily away from the boulder she'd been laying on. She thought—and hoped, too—that she was right about where the cabin was. If not, she might be lost for hours. Maybe days. Shit, she might even get lost in these woods forever.

A lump, cold as hail, formed in the pit of her stomach at the thought.

CHAPTER 43

"WE ARE HERE, investigating a possible cannibal hideout," Emeril said to the group as they marched toward the barn.

"You think he lives in a barn?" Fletcher asked drily.

Emeril shook his head and pointed at the farmhouse that was another fifty yards behind the barn. He was doing this for the college kids, but also for the camera. "If a cannibal lives in these woods, the likely place is over there."

Molly was walking ahead of them so that her camera was capturing footage of Emeril and the campers making their way to the barn, stepping backward to keep them in the shot. At the same time Emeril pointed and the campers turned their attention to the farmhouse, Molly turned around and pointed the camera at it. She zoomed in on the trees, even though she was afraid of what she might see. But the zoom-in didn't reveal anything except more details of the run-down farmhouse.

"Then why're we going to the barn?" It was Fred who asked.

"As an investigator," Emeril explained, "it is my duty to look into anything that seems peculiar."

They all knew what the old man was talking about and why he wanted to inspect the barn. The door on the structure looked newer than the rest of the damaged wood making up the structure. Fred and company hadn't seen the picture of the ear necklace dangling in the woods, so they didn't quite understand the consequences of what this might've meant the same way, but they knew something was odd about it.

"What do you think we'll find in there?" Vanessa asked. She and Brooke looked at one another and giggled nervously.

The story of the cannibal was nothing but fun and games for the campers. For now, anyway.

"I don't think anything. I make no assumptions. I just investigate," Emeril told her.

"Rad answer," Fletcher said, nodding in approval.

They reached the barn and stopped in front of it. Up close, the damage the structure suffered from the weather elements was more noticeable. Some of the wood had been waterlogged and was bumpy, while other spots (mainly on the roof) were milky white from having been bleached by the sun. Slick, bright green moss grew between the walls and the roof, and there was a musty smell hovering over the structure. None of them were sure if it was coming from inside or outside or both.

Maybe it was the isolation, but there was something more unnerving about this dilapidated barn than even the cabins behind them.

"Let's see what's behind door number one, shall we?" Emeril wished he hadn't made that joke. His nervous energy was showing through. He made a mental note to ask Molly to edit that out of the movie later.

He reached out to undo the lock on the barn door, but stopped halfway there when Molly shrieked.

Everyone turned to look at her as she dropped her camera. She was pointing out into the woods, her mouth agape. Almost in unison, they all diverted their attention to the spot her index finger was directing them to.

A figure, obscured by the shadows it stood under, stared back at them.

"What the fuck is that?" Fletcher yelled.

And then everything seemed to speed up before their eyes as the man emerged out of the woods, machete in his hand.

Nadine opened her eyes, waking up to the sound of people talking outside of the barn. She sat up, unbelieving.

It'd been so long since she'd heard anything other than rain pelting on the barn rooftop, animals scurrying around, her chains clanking, or her captor's voice, that the voices outside of the barn sounded like an alien language to her ears.

But it wasn't an alien language. It was English they were speaking. Plain, American English.

Nadine tightened her diaphragm, opened her mouth, and was about to scream to let the people know she was in here—when someone else, someone outside with them, beat her to the punch.

The scream was so loud and foreign to the quiet world she was used to that it hurt her eardrums. She clapped her hands over her ears, realizing that this unknown screaming was worse than the total silence.

Because the unknown sometimes brought danger with it.

The mask he was wearing was undoubtedly the face of someone else, covering his own face. The weapon he carried had flecks of dried blood on it from his latest victims. If this person approaching them wasn't a legitimate giant, then there was no such thing outside of mythology.

"RUN!" Fred screamed, and they did exactly that.

Except for Emeril, who fired at the maniac. The shots were wild and aimless and missed completely. Panic flooded him, then he too was running for his life.

They scattered in each and every direction. No one worried about maps or where they were heading or if they would get lost in the woods.

Survival was all they had on their mind.

She was here. Now that he was closer to the group, Ignacio saw her. Mamá's lookalike was here.

They ran like roaches scattering through a suddenly lit kitchen. Their bodies and clothes turned into blurs of color heading in a direction that they hoped would take them to safety. Whether it was distance from him or a spot that would hide them from his eyes, it didn't make a difference.

There was no way he was going to catch all of them, but that didn't matter. The only one that mattered was Mamá's lookalike.

She was running toward some trees east of the campgrounds, screaming at the top of her lungs, not realizing that her screaming would make it easier for him to follow her.

He took off running in that direction.

Behind him, he heard gunshots. Ignacio looked over his shoulder in time to see the old man start running away from him. Fear had made him give up on trying to kill Ignacio.

Good.

He was in the clear to chase Mamá's lookalike now.

"*Ven, ven! Vamos a jugar!*" he called after her, the words echoing through the woods: *Come, come. Let's play.*

Vanessa heard him huffing and puffing behind her as he chased her through the woods.

Why me? Why? she thought.

Her head felt light, like it was ready to pop. Her legs were turning to jelly with each step, but it wasn't from the exertion of the sprint. She ran regularly as part of her workout regimen; it was fear doing this to her. Hours of running a day, pushing through when she wanted to quit, eating salads for lunch, it all added up to nothing.

Fear trumped all.

Vanessa felt huge hands wrap around her neck, and then she was pulled down to the ground.

Ignacio grabbed her, her skin was so soft and smooth. It gave him a tingly feeling in his groin like he'd never felt before, but before he could get too excited, Varias Caras awoke.

We have to focus, estupido.

He pulled the girl down to the ground as hard as he could, then jumped on top of her, and squeezed her neck with both hands.

The girl stared up at him with almond colored eyes that were pleading, while her hands clawed at his arms to fight off the choke. Her nails dug deep enough to break his skin and draw blood, but that didn't do anything except anger Varias Caras.

Vanessa felt consciousness slipping out of her. Her scratching had done nothing. His grip hadn't loosened a bit—if anything, it'd gotten tighter—so instead she closed her eyes and waited to pass out.

It was better to do that than to continue to stare at this monster's soulless eyes behind the disgusting mask on his face.

The girl went limp. He took his hands off her throat and got up. She was sleeping, but not dead.

Good.

With her taken care of for now, he shifted his focus and listened for the sounds of the others. He heard them running through the woods. He could catch some of them if he hurried. None of them moved very fast.

But no, he had Mamá's lookalike. A good hunter knew when enough was enough. He'd let the others go. They didn't matter, anyway.

He picked up the girl and threw her over his shoulder, then headed for the barn. It was time to celebrate Mamá's birthday.

CHAPTER 44

THE STORIES OF the cannibal were true.

He was here in the flesh. A gargantuan man, wearing a mask made from the face of one of his victims. His long hair was a curly mess on his shoulders, his pants were filthy.

After missing his first shots, Emeril had run to hide behind a thicket of bushes, terrified by the reality of the situation. But he had his bearings back now, and knew the girl needed his help.

Emeril peeked over the bushes, and saw the cannibal putting Vanessa on his shoulders. It was too risky to take a shot from where he was—he might hit her, considering his poor aim. He had to get close enough that he wouldn't miss the cannibal. Maybe with the threat of the gun, he could persuade the maniac to put the girl down, and then shoot him in the chest. It was crazy, but he couldn't just run out of here and leave an innocent girl to die.

Emeril got out from behind the bushes and walked over to where he was, slowly inching toward the cannibal. Like some sort of illusion, he seemed to grow the closer Emeril got to him. But he had the upper hand, because in the excitement of catching his victim, the cannibal had his guard down. He didn't notice Emeril approaching him.

"Take your hands off the girl," he said, aiming the gun. He and the cannibal were about two arm's length away from each other.

Varias Caras finished putting the girl up on his shoulders like a fireman, and then turned around to face Emeril. His eyes grew big behind the mask when he saw the pistol pointed at him.

"Put her down," Emeril said again, trying to make it come out like a barked order, but there was a nervous quake at the end he couldn't hide.

"*Whaaa?*" Varias Caras said, kneeling down. With one arm, he started putting the girl down. Meanwhile, his free hand felt around the ground for the machete he'd put to the side. He did this while never taking his eyes off Emeril.

Emeril aimed at the cannibal's arm and pulled the trigger. But his hands trembled too much to aim properly, and he missed.

The bullet struck the ground a few inches from where Varias Caras' hand was. Grains of dirt flew up into a cloud. Varias Caras leapt up from his crouch and lunged forward with the speed of a panther.

Emeril shot again. The bullet struck the giant man in the shoulder, but it didn't stop him, so he fired again. The bullet tore through the cannibal's body near his ribs. Blood sprayed out from the wound and started leaking down his body, but the cannibal persisted.

Varias Caras swung the machete through the air. The blade went through the hand Emeril was holding the pistol with and chopped it right off at the wrist. The dismembered hand went through the air, an arc of blood following its trajectory before it hit the ground with a meaty thump.

Emeril screamed, and backed away, but the cannibal continued forward. He felt like a wall was about to collapse on top of him, and he knew death was imminent.

Varias Caras grabbed him by the throat and lifted him up into the air. Emeril tried to fight the grip off, but before he could lift his arm up, he was launched through the air at a tree. There was a thick, broken branch protruding out of the tree, with a sharp end like a javelin. The point went through Emeril's back and came out of his stomach. Several feet of his intestines were pulled out of his body as inertia slid him down the branch. They unraveled and hung from the tree like morbid vines.

When his momentum stopped, he still had enough life in him to be aware of what was happening. Emeril could see his blood and guts slicked on the branch coming out of his body and feel his legs dangling in the air. He felt like his body had been split in two, and he was becoming one with the tree. Then, he began to cough, and a torrent of blood poured out of his mouth.

Varias Caras approached him with the machete readied. He drove the blade down through the middle of Emeril's head, splitting it open. Emeril slumped over, dead. The tree branch was the only thing keeping his body from crashing to the ground.

Varias Caras pulled the machete out of his skull with a twist. There were a few pops, followed by the muddy sound of the blade dislodging from the skull.

Now that the rush of the kill was over, he felt the pain from the bullet wounds. He dropped the bloodied machete to the ground and fell to his knees.

Ignacio put his hand over the wound in his rib—the one that hurt the most—and felt the warm blood seep through the spaces of his fingers.

This was bad.

Stupid, stupid Ignacio. Why did he have to try to fight a man with a gun? He should've run.

He stayed there for a few seconds like a three-legged dog, with his right hand over the wound in his side, listening to his labored breathing. Wondering if he was going to live or not.

Le vantate, hijo. No te dejes.

Mamá. She was talking to him. Her spirit was near. He could feel her even closer than when he prayed to her head. She'd come to make sure her son was OK.

Ignacio was invigorated by this, and suddenly, the bullet wounds weren't as bad.

He picked himself up, bringing the machete with him, and strapped it to his back all in the same motion.

Then, he turned his focus back to the girl—and his heart nearly jumped out of his throat. She was gone.

Varias Caras dropped down to his knees and screamed at the top of his lungs.

The pain of having had Mamá's lookalike and losing her was worse than the bullet wounds.

"NO! NO! NO!"

Wildlife in the vicinity hearing his cries flew or scurried from their hiding spots in a mad dash to get away from whatever was making those awful, awful sounds.

CHAPTER 45

He was back on the normal trail, but the sound of the gun was loud enough that Gavin heard it. It made every hair on his body stand up. He turned around, and when he saw someone there, he almost screamed, but then he realized it was Brooke.

She was sprinting down the hidden path toward him, still several yards away, but even from this distance he knew something was wrong. Her skin was as pallid as used charcoal and she looked about ready to keel over and throw up at any second.

"Yo, Brooke, what's going on? Where're the others?" he shouted at her.

His first thought was that the old man and his accomplice had turned out to be perverts—but that didn't explain why Brooke was by herself.

It also didn't explain the gunshots, and he realized how stupid the thought was.

He stretched his neck out to see if maybe the others were in the distance coming behind her, but there was no one. Just Brooke.

Brooke was close enough now to hug him. She threw her arms around him and buried her face into his shoulder. She was dry heaving but held enough composure to talk. "Gav, we need to get the fuck out of here!"

"What's going on?" he said, putting his arms around her and bringing her close to him.

She shook her head. Something bad had happened. Gavin felt his balls begin to shrivel up into his body, and his mind raced with the worst thoughts possible, imagining the others had been shot dead.

"Some guy—this huge fucking guy—came out of the woods with a machete. We all ran… Oh, damnit Gav, we all should've left with you. Goddamnit."

"Whoa, whoa! Slow down, Brooke." Despite his words, the thoughts in his mind were coming faster now. "What're you talking about?"

"Emeril—that old man we met at the camp—he told us about this cannibal in the woods. And he's real, Gavin. He's real. He came running after us."

Gavin stepped back to examine her face. "A-are you shitting me?"

She shook her head. "We need to get the hell out of here."

"Where are the others?" Gavin said. He could hardly believe this.

"I don't know. We all just started running—he had a machete." Brooke broke into a sob, recounting it was too much for her to contain.

"We can't just leave them," Gavin said.

"Then you go back," she said, breaking away from him and starting down the path. "I'm getting out of here."

She meant she was going to take one of the cars back at the cabin and drive out of here. Which would leave just one escape vehicle for the rest of them. Noelle, Wayne, and Dalton could escape with Brooke. Gavin could go to the campgrounds and help the others fight off the cannibal.

Except, he had no fucking weapon on him.

He was trying to think this through quickly, knowing every second counted right now. With no weapon, if he returned to the campsite, he might be as good as dead. What would be the point of that?

If he went back to the cabin, he could find a weapon—the fire poker or the axe in the kitchen, for example—and then drive one of the vehicles to the camp. He'd mess up some grass and a bunch of bushes in the woods, but fuck nature.

His friends were in trouble.

Without wasting anymore time, he sprinted down the path in the same direction Brooke was going.

CHAPTER 46

VANESSA WASN'T SURE what happened between being yanked to the ground and waking up to Fletcher and Fred pulling her to her feet, but she knew they'd saved her life. With her holding onto them for support, the three of them ran as fast as they could through the woods.

Everything was blurry and spinning in Vanessa's vision and she could barely feel her legs underneath her. The back of her head throbbed in the spot that had struck the ground.

They climbed over a huge, fallen oak tree and Fletcher told her to lay down. For a moment, the three of them sat on the grass, trying to suck in air into their lungs as quietly as they could.

Fred caught his breath first, and then raised up into a crouch to peer over the top of the tree trunk. The grass underneath him rustled at an alarming volume, but really, any sound was alarming given the situation.

His head cleared the tree just enough for him to see the area ahead. There were no signs of the cannibal, and the hope in his heart that the gunshots had been the killer getting gunned down strengthened.

"Any signs of him?" Fletcher whispered, too worried about making noise to get up to look for himself.

Fred shook his head. "No. Nothing."

Satisfied with that answer, Fletcher said to Vanessa, "Are you okay?"

"Head hurts, but other than that, I'm okay... I'll be okay."

They were speaking in whispers that were just audible. Fletcher went to get up to look where Fred was looking but stopped when in front of him, he saw a figure approaching them from the trees.

No fucking way, Fletcher thought, feeling a hot wetness at the front of his crotch. He screamed.

Fred turned, saw the cannibal coming out of the woods, and started running. The others ran, too.

The chase was on once again.

Vanessa ran into an area thick with thin trees and scruffy bushes, her strategy was to get lost behind the wildly growing foliage. But she hadn't considered that the overgrown plants would make seeing the ground difficult. The front of her shoe struck an unseen root protruding out of the ground. Her ankle twisted from the sudden stop, while the rest of her body kept falling forward. Vanessa yelped like a chihuahua that had just gotten kicked. She stuck her arms out to keep from faceplanting into the ground.

The stumble gave Varias Caras enough time to catch up to her. He grabbed her by the ankle with one hand. With his other hand, he swung the machete down at her leg.

She screamed—this time it was a loud, from deep down inside type of scream—as the blade chopped her leg off from the shin down.

Ignacio stomped on her back to keep her from moving away. Vanessa screamed again, not just from the pain but from the fear. She screamed so loud that she began to throw up. The morning's breakfast burrito and a deluge of bile poured out of her mouth.

Using both hands, Varias Caras raised the machete over his head and then brought it down on her other leg. One whack was all it took, and the girl's leg was hacked off at relatively the same spot as the first. The cut veins spurted blood all over Ignacio's arms. It was hot and sticky and tickled against his skin. It tickled so much he let out a small giggle.

Meanwhile, Vanessa howled in pain one last time, dug her nails into the earth, and then her eyes rolled to the back of her head as she lost consciousness.

"I am sorry," Ignacio said, staring at the bloodbath on the grass left from his hacking job. "But this is what happens to bad Barbies."

Ignacio took off one of her pink Converse sneakers. They were tiny to him, like a little doll's shoe—a Barbie's shoe, if you will. He put it in the back pocket of his pants. He would present it to her later, after cleaning the splatters of blood from it, to make her feel more comfortable in the barn.

To make her feel welcomed.

With one arm, Ignacio scooped her up. She was much lighter now. He carried her to a tree nearby, leaving a trail of blood behind them. Ignacio hung her onto a sturdy-looking branch from the collar of her shirt. He tugged on her waist to make sure she was on there securely. She was.

Satisfied, Varias Caras started off through the woods. He was going to hunt them down and kill them all before they could come back and take his Barbie away from him again.

No way was he going to let that happen a second time. Ignacio was a dummy, but he wasn't *that* big of a dummy.

Ignacio closed his eyes and focused his hearing to locate the others. He could hear two of them running. He could hear their shoes beating against the ground as they ran. Hear the leaves rustling and twigs swaying as they blew past them. It was like the trees…no, like the woods themselves were on his side, whispering where the prey was to him.

He located three of them. One of them had just gone through a window of one of the cabins. He could hear the kid's elevated heartbeat. It was faint, but there was no rhythm like that of a panicked human heartbeat.

A second one had just fired up a car. That one was going to get away, but that was OK, there was nothing he could do about that.

The third one was closer, running through the trees. He was slowing down, though, and Ignacio knew which way to go to cut him off.

He started after this one first.

These next ones weren't like Ignacio's Barbie. These he was going to kill for the thrills. Varias Caras took full control of the reigns now.

Vanessa's screams echoed throughout the forest. Each one was worse than the last, and each one twisting his stomach up into a tighter knot. Fred couldn't contain it anymore, he had to stop.

It was a one-two punch of imagining what was happening to Vanessa and the strain from sprinting that made Fred drop to his knees and vomit. The retching came all the way from the very bottom of his stomach. It came out so violently and strong that his head felt like it was going to burst.

Fred finished throwing up with a cough and wiped the saliva and throw-up from his mouth with the back of his hand.

The worst wasn't over for Fred Meyers yet, though.

Out the corner of his eye, he saw Varias Caras coming after him through the trees. He must've taken some shortcut—

again—or maybe he was a ghost (*hadn't the old man mentioned something about ghosts?*). Fred forced himself to start running on wobbly legs, feeling like he was going to fall over at any moment.

Varias Caras powerwalked after him. The kid must have found a second wind, because he was moving quickly now. It was time to change tactics. He took the knife out from his back pocket, aimed it at his leg, and launched it through the air.

The blade went through the back of Fred's knee, and immediately took his leg out from under him.

"AH! FUCK!" Fred yelled, dropping down to his good knee. He reached around to pull the knife out from his leg.

Varias Caras leapt forward and grabbed Fred by the shirt before the kid realized it. He lifted him into the air with both hands.

The kid was light—not as light as the Barbie, but light enough for him to pick him up over his head like he was a pro weightlifter. Then, Varias Caras did a motion similar to a forward lunge, so that his knee was bent, and at the same time slammed the boy down onto his knee, back first.

Fred's spine snapped, and he died instantly. Varias Caras let the boy's deadweight roll off his knee. He got up, pulling the knife from the dead kid's leg as he did so.

Varias Caras closed his eyes and focused his ears to locate the others. This close to the campgrounds, his super hearing was even more extraordinary. He could hear the heartbeat of the camper hiding in the cabin. The others were further away, almost inaudible to him. He probably wouldn't be able to catch them.

Oh well. Not like it mattered too much. There were enough dead bodies to feed him for weeks already, and he was going to kill the one hiding at the camp, too.

Varias Caras kept his ears homed on the camper's heartbeat as he trudged toward the cabins, noticing that the pace was slowing. The person must've felt safe in their hiding spot. But in a matter of moments, they wouldn't feel that safety anymore.

Fletcher found himself in one of the larger cabins that had multiple rooms, hiding underneath a bed. His skin was crawling from sharing a space with a bunch of dust bunnies and rodent droppings, but it was better than being exposed.

He could barely remember how he ended up here. One minute he was watching the cannibal coming out of the woods after them, the next he was in this cabin looking for a hiding spot.

The bed seemed as perfect a hiding spot as possible. It was in the middle of the room, so that if the cannibal came in through the front door, he could slip out the side closest to the window and jump out of it. If he came in through the window (which Fletcher had already opened in preparation for scenario number one), then he would slip out the other side of the bed and run out the front door.

The more his heart slowed to a regular rhythm, the more convinced he was this was a solid plan of survival. Shit, he might not even need it. The killer might not be able to find him and give up looking for him.

He couldn't remember if the guy was chasing him or Fred or Vanessa, but he knew they'd all ran in different directions. That much he did recall; looking over his shoulder and seeing the other two running deeper into the woods.

By how it seemed, their assailant hadn't come after him. He'd been under this bed for a while—fifteen minutes, maybe less or maybe more. Time didn't exactly operate the same when you were in danger of being murdered.

The only thing he was sure of was the quietness that surrounded him. Some bugs buzzed their songs in the bushes outside, but besides that, he hadn't heard a thing. No leaves rustling or grass being moved. Not even birds in the trees or a mouse running around.

It was a stillness so prominent that it seemed to have stopped time. Fletcher wondered if when he finally crawled out from underneath this bed, and went back to the real world, if it would be years in the future. He wondered if maybe he'd found some magical spot in the woods where time operated differently than the rest of the universe.

A loud bang at the front of the cabin made these stoner thoughts disperse from Fletcher's mind. He realized he wasn't as safe as he thought.

Before he could crawl from underneath the bed and escape out of the window as he'd been planning, he heard heavy, quick footfalls just outside the room he was in.

The heartbeat got louder and louder the further he walked down the short corridor. Whenever Ignacio was searching for prey, it reminded him of playing Hide 'N' Go Seek with the neighborhood kids when he was a child and how good he was at it. That'd been when he was really little, back before he or the other kids realized he was different. Before they stopped playing games with him and started calling him names like "big retard" or "*tonto*" if they knew Spanish.

Just like the kids back then, his prey didn't realize Ignacio's ability to hear better than anyone else. They thought their hiding spots were good, and maybe they were, if they were hiding from anyone other than him.

The stakes were different when hunting and playing Hide 'N' Go Seek, of course. Finding the neighborhood kids meant winning a game. Finding prey meant food.

But the rush? The rush was just the same.

Varias Caras entered the room the hiding camper was in. He could hear his heartbeats coming from underneath the bed. To Ignacio's ear it was as loud as someone hammering a nail into the floorboards.

He heard the kid move, then rethink his movement, and stop.

Varias Caras trudged over to the bed, hearing the pace of his victim's heartbeats increasing with each second. It was these moments that Varias Caras lived for. The surge of power that coursed through him before murdering someone was like nothing else. When he looked into his victims' eyes and saw them pleading for mercy, when they were shaking in fear of his presence, when they screamed for their lives, he felt like a god.

Varias Caras crouched down and reached under the bed to pull the kid out—but his hand clasped around air. The kid had summoned up some courage at the last second and slipped out the other side of the bed.

Varias Caras hopped to his feet. The kid was running for the open window.

"You like window?!" Ignacio yelled at him.

He jumped through the air, clearing the bed and the space between him and the kid in one giant leap. He wrapped his arms around Fletcher.

Fletcher kicked at the air, and threw a punch over his head at Varias Caras, but there was no power to it. It was nothing more than a glancing blow.

Varias Caras picked him up off his feet, and suplexed him head first onto the floor. Stars exploded in Fletcher's vision, and his limbs uselessly went limp as he laid on the ground.

Varias Caras went over to the window and closed it shut. Then, he went back to Fletcher, and lifted him up off the floor by his waistband with two hands. He swung his arms back, and then launched Fletcher at the window.

Fletcher went headfirst through the glass. Shards cut his body open as the rest of him flew through the broken window and landed outside the cabin a crumpled, bleeding mess.

Ignacio opened the window and climbed out of it. He took his time, knowing full well his prey was wounded and had no fight in him.

He grabbed Fletcher by the hair. The kid's useless legs dragged across the grass as Ignacio pulled him to the window. Ignacio balanced the kid's neck on the sill, so that his head was inside the cabin, but the rest of his body was outside.

The odd positioning woke something in Fletcher up, and he came to.

"Wh-what are you doing…? NO, NO, NO!" Fletcher pleaded. He realized what was going to happen and started thrashing his arms and legs.

But it did him no good, because Ignacio was pressing against his back with one strong arm that felt like a boulder was crushing him. Even if he had all his strength in him, Fletcher didn't think he'd be able to budge from underneath him. He closed his eyes and waited for it to be over.

"I like window, too!" Ignacio laughed, then with his free hand slammed the window closed as hard as he could.

Ignacio's strength forced the window to act like a guillotine, and Fletcher's neck was split in half. His head hit the cabin floor with a hollow thud like someone dropping a head of cabbage, while his body slumped onto the grass outside.

Ignacio danced around in a circle, clapping his hands over his head. The old man was dead. The two boys who had been with the Barbie were dead. He couldn't get the woman or the other girl in their group, but that was OK.

He had the Barbie.

It was time to celebrate Mamá's birthday.

CHAPTER 47

The area around the cabin was quiet, but now that Noelle was looking into the den through the very same window she'd escaped from, she knew why.

She followed the splatters of dark, drying blood with her eyes and saw the first head laying on the ground by the pool table.

Dalton stared up at the ceiling, an expression of pained agony from Ignacio's punch frozen on his face. His blue hair was turning purple because of the blood that had seeped and mixed in with the dye. Next to the head was his body. The back of the flannel shirt, like his hair, was drenched from the pool of blood.

She spotted the second head further into the room, by one of the walls. Even though this head was face down, she knew it belonged to Wayne. A pang of guilt struck her heart as her empty words of telling him they'd be OK echoed in her mind. She wanted to crumple to the ground and cry, but she knew she had to stay strong if she was going to survive this.

Then, she heard sobs coming from the woods. Sobs that were loud enough to be confused with screams, and she turned to see Brooke coming up the path she and the others had used to go into the woods earlier. It had been just this morning, but it felt like that'd happened an eon ago.

Mascara ran down Brooke's cheeks in dark rivulets. Something had happened in the woods, and something told Noelle it had to do with the man who'd murdered Dalton and Wayne.

"Brooke!" Noelle called to her.

She looked over at the side of the cabin where Noelle stood and then shuffled toward her. They met at the front of the vehicles and threw their arms around each other.

"Brooke, what happened?" Noelle asked.

"A crazy guy came out of the woods," Brooke buried her head into Noelle's shoulder and cried harder. After a few seconds of that, she raised her head up. "And then there were gunshots. Oh God, it was awful—Where's Dalton?"

Noelle shook her head. "He—he didn't make it, Brooke."

"What do you mean?" Brooke let go of her and stepped back, her eyes huge. "What do you mean he didn't make it?"

She sucked in a deep breath and was ready to tell her it all in one go, when over her shoulder Noelle saw Gavin racing out of the woods.

Unlike Brooke's face, his was full of color. It was a red that was somehow pale and vibrant at the same time, like the color of a cherry-bomb firecracker.

"What're you two doing!" he yelled at the girls. "We've gotta get going!"

Gavin ran past them without slowing down.

"Gavin, stop!" Noelle yelled, and started after him.

He'd hopped over the porch steps in one hurried leap and was at the top of them when he stopped and turned to Noelle. "What? Where're the others? Where's Wayne?"

"He didn't make it, Gav," Noelle said, using the same phrase as she had telling Brooke about her cousin. "I'm sorry…"

Gavin shook his head, and his face contorted with emotion. "What the fuck are you talking about, Noelle? Didn't make—?"

It hit him. Hit him like a sledgehammer to his heart.

Noelle knew his pain very well, but she needed answers. "What happened in the woods?"

Ignoring her question, Gavin sprinted into the cabin.

"Gav! Wait!" Noelle called, but it was too late.

"They're dead, aren't they?" Brooke said. "Dalton and Wayne…they're dead."

"Yes, Brooke. They are." Noelle's shoulders slumped. "We got attacked by a man with a machete."

"The cannibal," Brooke said, and suddenly the temperature outside turned freezing cold.

"Cannibal? What're you talking about?"

"We met an old man in the woods." Brooke had calmed, maybe because she was in some sort of autopilot mode from the shock of hearing her cousin was dead, but she wasn't blubbering her words anymore. "Said something about a cannibal out in the woods. Wanted us to be in some movie him and a girl he was with are making."

"Okay," Noelle said, somewhat following. "Then what?"

"Gavin got pissed before all that, though, and went back through the woods himself. The rest of us stayed to be in the movie, and we were walking to this barn out in the woods when the cannibal showed up. I ran back here and found Gavin on the trail and now…now…they might all be dead?"

Noelle was too stunned to respond.

Brooke gulped, then continued. "We have to get out of here, Noelle."

"What about the others? Did you see what happened to them?"

"No. I think they all ran a different direction. I don't know what happened to them, but we heard gunshots." Brooke pointed her chin toward the cabin. "I think he wants to take one of the cars back to the camp to help them."

Noelle felt her head spinning. There was so much going on, so much to take in. She wasn't sure what was happening or what would happen. But one thing she was certain about was that they were in danger out here.

Gunshots. A maniac wielding a machete. Dead bodies in the cabin. None of this was good.

Brooke started for the cabin. Noelle followed, worried about what condition Gavin would be in when they found him.

He sprinted through the cabin, not caring about anything. Not caring if a whole cannibal family was in there wielding chainsaws, ready to cut him up and turn him into their next meal. In that moment, he felt he could run through them. Run through anything.

He went into the den. At the far wall he saw his little brother's head, stupid mop-top he'd always given him grief about and all.

It looked fake detached from the body that was always wearing a video game themed or Mountain Dew t-shirt. It looked like plastic.

It wasn't Wayne's, it couldn't have been.

This was a joke from the others to get him back for being a shithead. Everything about it had been a setup. Fletcher finding the map, running into the movie makers in the woods. The story about the cannibal.

Yeah, that had to be it. This was some elaborate joke.

They wanted to see him on the verge of tears. Everyone would pop out from their hiding spots and come into the den to laugh at him. Wayne would pick up the plastic head, duck his real head into his shirt, and laugh at him for thinking he'd been decapitated by a crazed killer.

This was payback for him being an asshole to them all these years.

A big scare.

(*Ha-ha, real funny guys!*)

They'd all laugh at his expense, and really, he wouldn't be mad. He deserved it, and after the initial embarrassment he would laugh, too.

The old man and the woman, they were probably some sort of professional pranksters. He'd seen some of those people on YouTube before.

Yeah, it made sense. There was no way that was Wayne's head laying by the wall over there. That's why it was face down, so it looked more convincing. He'd flip it over and there wouldn't even be a face on it, that's how fake it was.

The others would come out soon, pointing and making fun of him, like some fucked up reverse surprise party where the goal isn't a nice gesture for the person. Instead, the goal was to make the person's knees weak and get them to feel all of the pain they'd inflicted on anyone in their life reflected back at them.

And it worked. Their stupid prank worked like a charm, or a curse, whatever, because Gavin fell to his knees and felt as if someone had reached into his chest and pulled his heart out.

He waited…waited for the reveal of the joke to come.

But it never came.

He cried harder than he'd ever cried in his life. He closed his eyes, but his little brother's decapitated head was burned into his mind's eye, and it was all he could see behind the darkness of his eyelids.

CHAPTER 48

Molly was driving the Subaru down the road they'd taken to get to Camp Slaughter. She was maybe a mile out from the campgrounds. Maybe two. Maybe only half a mile. There was no way for her to tell, these damn woods all looked the same.

The moment the cannibal showed up, the beauty and the serenity she'd been appreciating when they first entered the woods had vanished. After hearing the first screams of someone being murdered by him, the woods became a labyrinthine nightmare for her.

She stopped the car and buried her face in her hands, resting her elbows against the steering wheel. She didn't cry, but she just sat there in that position for a good while, taking in deep breaths to try to get ahold of herself. It wasn't a time for emotions right now, it was time to think things through.

She could continue driving, get out and find safety. Call for help or find it somewhere. Hadn't there been a police station or something a few miles before they'd found Camp Slaughter? Maybe not. Maybe that was a false memory being recreated by her heart's desires, or something like that.

This whole mess was confusing.

The one thing she was certain about was that she'd left Emeril behind. She'd seen him going the opposite way she ran—the *wrong* way by all accounts—straight toward where the cannibal was going.

That idiot, she thought.

But she'd heard a gunshot go off. It'd been his pistol. Had to have been. A flicker of hope stirred in her that he was alive.

If he was, the right thing to do would be to turn back to help him.

And if anyone else had gotten away—shit, for all she knew the college kids could have been packing and gunned down the cannibal themselves—they would need an escape vehicle, too.

Molly turned the key in the ignition, firing the Subaru's engine back on. The engine starting up sounded like a lion's roar, and it helped to psych her up for what she was about to do.

Molly flipped a bitch on the road and started back to Camp Slaughter, flooring the accelerator.

She hadn't fired a gun in ages—at least ten years—but she assumed it was just like riding a bicycle. A skill that once you acquired you never unlearned.

Aim, shoot, and kill. It would be that easy. She hoped.

The new Barbie was still hanging from the tree where he'd left her. Her eyes closed, her breathing slowing down. He needed to get her back to the barn and her wounds cleaned up soon.

Ignacio unhooked her from the tree branch, then slumped her over his shoulder like a sandbag. Blood dripped to the ground from her injured legs as he took her back to the barn.

In the barn he had supplies he would use to cauterize the wound, bandage her up, and then wake her to start the party.

This had become a messier job than he'd hoped for. The thought occurred to him that the blood was leaving behind a trail straight to him and where he kept his toys, but that was fine. He'd come back to wash it off the grass when he was done fixing up the new Barbie.

He didn't think either of the girls who'd gotten away would be coming back. They'd been terrified when they ran away. And the police wouldn't be here for a good while—if ever. They might not even be able to find the place.

Not a lot of people came by the campgrounds.

Ignacio pulled the barn doors open. The old Barbie had moved into the darkest corner that her chains allowed her to, but he could see the yellow glow of her eyes peering back at him. Could sense her fear in the air, too.

He stuck his tongue out past the mouth hole of the mask and licked the air. Sweet, and ripe. A hollowness began to grow in his heart at the thought he would slaughter her at the end of the night.

Varias Caras walked through the barn and placed the new Barbie on the floor near the chains he'd set up yesterday. The new Barbie was out cold, not a muscle moving. There was no point in restraining her just yet.

Ignacio took the box of matches out of his pants, lit one, and then went over to light the torches. He'd need light to fix the new Barbie up.

While her captor was rummaging through a rusty filing cabinet where he kept medical supplies, Nadine stared at the young girl. The girl's legs had been cut off, just how her feet had been. Except this was worse, because her legs were cut off from the middle of the shins down. Blood gushed out of the holes with no signs of stopping, and Nadine wondered if the girl was going to stay alive much longer.

The thought made her cry. She tried to stifle it by pressing her lips together, but that did nothing. She sobbed and heaved at seeing the poor girl laying there, out cold. This was worse than she'd imagined it would be.

Then, ice-cold fingers of fear clutched around her heart tighter as she wondered what that meant for her. Her crying grew louder and more rapid, and she was sure that it was going to set Varias Caras off the deep end as it had before.

But it didn't do anything. The most attention of his it drew was that he glanced away from the cabinet he was rummaging through, then he went back to his task.

He had a new toy, a new Barbie. He didn't care about Nadine anymore.

I'm old, Nadine thought. *Old toys get thrown out.*

She gulped, looked over at the machete on his back—still stained with blood from his last victims, no doubt.

Nadine felt another touch from fear's hands. This one wrapped around her throat, and squeezed it shut, as she realized she would be dead soon enough.

CHAPTER 49

"Gav, come on. Let's go," Noelle pleaded.

Outside the cabin, they heard Brooke start up Fletcher's Jeep. She hadn't even bothered to come into the den to see her cousin. She scooped the keys up from the kitchen counter and ran back outside to escape out of the woods. While doing this, she'd called into the den to Noelle and Gavin telling them she was going to call the police the moment her cell phone had service and kept reminding them that they were free to come with her.

Noelle silently turned down her offer, because the guilt of running away and leaving Wayne and Dalton to die still crushed her. She needed to be *valiant*, as Rachel had said.

She wasn't going to let Gavin go back to the camp by himself and get killed. At the very least she was going to try to convince him to escape out of here with her in the other vehicle. But before that could happen, she needed him to get control of himself.

He was sitting on the floor, hunched over and crying into his hands. Noelle was kneeling over him and rubbing his shoulders. Everything she'd tried to get him to compose himself had failed. Really, though, there was nothing that would have worked, because there was nothing that could fix the grief of seeing the remains of a loved one's murder.

Then it happened suddenly. Gavin stopped crying. From full-throttle weeping to zero in an instant. He shook his head, rubbed his puffy eyes, and sighed. "I'm going back to the camp."

"No, Gav," Noelle argued. "Think about this. Brooke told me what happened, the same cannibal did this—"

"I don't care. I'm going." He brushed Noelle's hands off his shoulders and got to his feet. "You can't stop me, so shut up. Go with Brooke if you're scared."

"It's no time to be a tough guy, Gavin," Noelle said, getting in front of him.

"Out of my way, Noelle." There was an edge to his voice. "I'm going back to kill this fucker myself."

"You don't have a weapon."

They heard the Jeep's tires crunching on the gravel outside the window as Brooke pulled out of the driveway. The sound got fainter and fainter as Brooke escaped, leaving them with only one car.

"I'll find a weapon," Gavin said, and started walking around her.

"What if he's already dead? What if the gunshots you heard meant someone killed him? We'd just be wasting time."

"Then I'll piss on his corpse," Gavin said. He needed to quench his thirst for revenge in any way possible.

"We should let the police handle this. Think this through. I know you're mad and everything, but just stop and think."

"You think he stopped and thought about killing my little brother, Noelle?" Gavin had been walking out of the room but stopped at the doorway. He turned to face her. His eyes were red and puffy, but a darkness hovered over his face. "I guess you wouldn't know, since you ran away and left him and Dalton to die, though, right?"

"Th-that's not fair, Gav. I was scared…I…I didn't know what to do. I panicked…"

"Yeah, well, *I* know what I'm doing."

"You're going to get yourself killed!"

"If that cannibal doesn't kill me, my parents will, anyway."

Noelle wasn't sure if she imagined it or if it actually happened, but she saw a smirk flash across his face. And it was that phrase, that moment, that made her realize just how young they truly were.

"There're knives in the kitchen," Gavin told her, continuing out of the room. "Grab one and meet me by the car. Or stay here, or whatever you're going to do."

CHAPTER 50

The blood and the bodies told Molly everything she needed to know. She was the last survivor.

She saw Emeril first. He was about five feet off the ground, hanging from a tree branch that had pierced through his abdomen. Gravity had slumped him over to the right side, and his neck was bent so his head rested against his shoulder on an angle that would have been uncomfortable if he were alive. The blood around the gaping hole in his stomach was turning into a thick, maroon crust.

Several yards away from where her business partner had been turned into a human shish-kabob was one of the college kids. It was the scrawny one, the one who'd gotten into an argument with the muscled kid. His back was bent in half, and one didn't need to be an expert in anatomy to know his spinal cord was snapped—most likely in several places. It was like something out of a possession horror movie, where the director shows the audience how much the demon has taken over by twisting the person into unnatural positions. Only this wasn't special effects or a camera trick. This was an actual person's body curved into a "U."

Molly felt an uneasiness in her stomach. This was her first time seeing a murder scene, or dead bodies for that matter, and it was gruesome. But she had to stay strong. Now was not a time for weakness.

She started for the barn, wishing her plan of finding the cannibal out in the open and running him over would've worked, but he was nowhere to be found.

She was going to have to do this the old fashioned way. The most dangerous way, and probably the stupidest way, too. She'd have to approach him and kill him with Emeril's revolver.

At the front of the barn there was a trail of blood leading past the doors, which meant the cannibal had at the very least gone inside at some point. She hoped some of the blood she was seeing belonged to him. Maybe he'd retreated in there because he was badly wounded. And maybe it would be as easy as shooting him in the head from point blank.

She couldn't go in just yet, though. It wouldn't be smart to just barge in.

Better to investigate around some more. It was her own voice giving her the advice, but it was a skill she'd learned from Emeril. He'd always made sure to investigate what was in plain sight before barging in through any doors.

Clues could be anywhere.

Molly traced another trail of blood. It took her through a tangle of weeds and thorny branches that made small cuts on her shins that she ignored. The bloody trail led her to the oak tree Vanessa had been hanging from. The girl wasn't there, of course, but the pools of blood from her hacked off legs were, nearly touching to form one bigger puddle.

Molly looked up the tree, expecting to see a dead body dangling, but saw nothing.

To her, this confirmed where the cannibal was. Or at the very least, where he'd been after having killed Emeril and Fred. Maybe he'd just stored the body into the barn and then gone back to wherever the hell he stayed permanently.

She considered this as she doubled back to the barn, back through the irritating thorns cutting at her shins.

This is nothing compared to the pain Emeril must've felt, she thought, with a pang of both guilt and pain ringing in her heart.

She got to the barn and froze, realizing the enormity of the task.

The cannibal might be in there. She knew he'd gone through at least three people in a matter of minutes, and here she was with just a revolver, about to take him on herself.

Molly shook her head to rid the doubt out of it. She could do this. He was a human, nothing more.

A bullet to his head or his heart would end it. All he'd been wearing was a vest, cargo pants, boots, and that disgusting mask on his face. No body armor she could remember.

Then again, she'd only caught a glimpse of him.

But still. The leather mask, as scary as it was and as long as it might haunt her nightmares, wouldn't protect him from a bullet.

An image of Emeril hanging skewered from the tree branch flashed into her head, and anger pushed past her fear.

Molly drew the gun out of her pocket and checked the cylinder to make sure it was loaded. All six bullets were in there. She snapped the cylinder back into place, gripped the handle tight with one hand, and with the other she threw the barn door's latch open.

CHAPTER 51

He floored the accelerator, but the Honda wouldn't go any further. Its engine was too weak, and the frame was too low for it to push past the tangle of bushes under it. Gavin slammed his fist on the side of the steering wheel.

"FUCK!" he screamed. "FUCK! FUCK!"

His plan to drive back to Camp Slaughter wasn't going to work. The face of the salesman who'd sold him the car, who'd promised ice-cold AC and great gas mileage from the Honda, flashed into his mind and he hated him in that moment.

But that quickly faded away, because he knew the car salesman had nothing to do with what was happening. It was Gavin's fault. All his fault, and only his fault. No one else had even wanted to come on this stupid trip. He'd practically had to beg his best friend to come, for fuck's sake.

Come on Fredster, it's our last summer before we turn into boring adults. Let's do it big. And all Fred wanted to do was hang out with this girl in the passenger seat next to him who for some reason had gone along with his crazy (now failed) plan.

If it wasn't for him, for him and his stupid fucking ideas, Noelle and Fred wouldn't even be here. They'd be back in the burbs, maybe getting ice cream or having a picnic at some park. They'd be somewhere safe. Somewhere where cannibals didn't chase you through the woods to cut your head off and weird old men didn't ask you to be in their YouTube videos.

He'd done this to all of them. Noelle, Fred, Fletcher, Wayne, Brooke, Vanessa, Brooke's cousin. It was his fault they all got caught up in this shit. His mind wasn't letting itself entertain that others might be dead by now, not just his little brother and Dalton, because the guilt of having brought them out here into this situation was enough.

"Gav, we have to figure something else out," Noelle said, forcing herself to hold onto braveness that was quickly fading. "We're wasting time just sitting here."

He lifted his head off the steering where he'd rested it in frustration. "Yeah, you're right… But what? What can we do?"

"I—I don't know… Something. Anything…" She didn't finish her sentence, but Gavin had an idea what she wanted to say.

Anything was better than sitting here, waiting for the cannibal to come kill them and eat them—

Something popped into his head. The old man and the woman, they'd come into Camp Slaughter in a Subaru. That meant there was a way to get to the campgrounds by car.

Gavin threw the car into reverse, and then floored the accelerator. The bushes it was on top of sprung up to their regular size as the car shot back into the dirt trail. They hadn't gotten far down the path before they were stopped, so it wouldn't take long for them to return to Lakewood Cabin.

"Gavin, what're you doing?" The suddenness of this reversal worried Noelle that his plan B was even crazier than plan A.

"The old man and the woman. They drove into the camp. I'm going to see if I can find the road they took to get there. I remember which way they came in from, so I think I can find it."

I did say "anything," Noelle thought, sitting back in the car seat. She took in a deep breath, letting the smell of pine trees and honeysuckles coming through the window fill her nostrils. Clutching the ax she got from the cabin tight against her chest, she wondered if this was the last time she'd ever smell summer again.

CHAPTER 52

Varias Caras was using a pair of tweezers to pull out the bullet lodged into his shoulder. It hadn't gone in too deep because his shoulder bone had stopped it, but it was in there nice and snug. He had to wiggle it around like a loose tooth to get it to start coming out. He let out short grunts of pain as he pulled the bullet out of the wound.

It came out slicked with blood, and hurt on its way out more than it had going in. Most of that had to do with the adrenaline of his hunting wearing off, but to Ignacio it was all the same. He dropped the bullet to the barn floor. It clattered, and rolled, leaving little red stains in its wake.

Luckily for Ignacio, that was the only bullet he had to deal with. The one that had gotten him around the ribs had torn through his body. He'd have to bandage the wound up, so he'd stop leaking blood everywhere, but that was it.

Before he could go over to where the medical supplies were to take care of that, he heard the barn door opening behind him.

Someone was here. He hadn't heard the person coming to the barn because he'd had his guard down again. *Estupido.*

Ignacio turned around. The silhouette standing in the doorway was thin and hunched over, in a posture that suggested they were uncertain of what they were doing. And scared, too.

Ignacio could hear the person's heart beating in his ears now that he was focused on it. It beat loudly and fast.

Ignacio's own heart started to beat rapidly when he saw the outline of the gun in the person's hand.

"W-w-who there!?" Ignacio shouted.

Behind him, Nadine screamed as if in response to his question, but what made her scream was the same concern Ignacio had. The gun. A gun meant bullets would start flying while she was out here in the open; immobilized and unable to duck for cover.

"Who there? Tell me who there!" Ignacio's lips quivered.

The person walked into the barn, getting lost in the pocket of darkness between the sunlight coming in through the open door and the torchlights.

Ignacio felt his heart speeding up, and the barn walls getting smaller. He wondered if this was how his prey felt before he killed them.

He opened his mouth to ask the question a third time but stopped himself as Molly stepped just short of arm's length. The torchlight shined over the revolver's metal.

Ignacio swallowed. The barrel was pointed right at his chest. She was going to kill him.

On Mamá's birthday.

He had to act quick. He threw the tweezers at her since it was the only thing he had in his hands, and Molly pulled the trigger.

At the last minute, her aim was thrown off and the bullet hit him in the shoulder—the same one that was already damaged, but that didn't stop him. He jumped forward and grabbed Molly by the wrist of the hand holding the gun. Ignacio squeezed as hard as he could until he felt the wrist bone break.

Molly screamed and dropped the revolver.

Nadine saw the shiny, metal object falling out of the woman's hands as Varias Caras attacked her. It slid across the floor, as if it were on a track, as if destiny itself were pulling it closer to her. She couldn't believe her eyes when it finally stopped, and she got a good look at the object.

It was a revolver.

She crawled over to it, but the chains stopped her a few inches short of it. There was still some slack to them, though, and as she reached out, she pulled hard on her restraints. The metal cuffs dug into her skin, but it worked.

Her hand curled around the gun. And it felt like the world was right once again.

Varias Caras had Molly in a bearhug and lifted her up off her feet. She felt like she was suddenly in a vice made of flesh that smelled like meat and grease. Molly tried kicking at his genitals, but without seeing where she was aiming, it was useless.

Ignacio flexed his arms. There was a series of pops as bones broke in her body. Molly felt her ribcage shatter, and then her body felt like it was closing in on itself. Her organs felt like they were about to pop out of the nearest orifice.

Then, Varias Caras relieved some of the pressure, only to pump his arms as hard as he could again.

Crack. Pop. Snap.

This time it was the disks in her spine that made the noise as they were dislodged from the column and broke at the same time.

Molly's eyes rolled to the back of her head, her legs stopped kicking, her arms stopped clawing at his mask. She was dead.

Ignacio dropped her to the ground and fell back on his ass. He was out of breath, scared, hurt, and bleeding.

Behind him, the old Barbie continued to scream at the top of her lungs.

Too much noise! Too much noise!

He got up, and ran over to the wall, smashing his head into it as hard as he could to try to drown out the sound and shake out the bad thoughts in his head, but it was no good. All he did was manage to make his head hurt.

He pounded his fists against the wall and screamed—adding to the noise, adding to his anger.

Mamá's birthday was ruined.

Nadine's screams were only a bluff to get him to come close enough for her to shoot him, but she hadn't expected him to charge the wall head first at full speed.

The impact shook the entire barn, and for a second Nadine thought she'd fucked up and the whole structure was about to collapse on top of both of them.

Please don't, please!

God must have been hearing her pleas, because the barn stayed intact.

Varias Caras had fallen to his knees, but he was still conscious and started getting up to his feet. Nadine reached behind her, where she'd put the revolver to keep it hidden until she was ready to use it. She felt the cool metal in her hands.

This was going to be tricky. She would only have one shot to kill him.

A Hail Mary.

But her weapon this time was better than a porcelain lamp.

Her throat felt like sandpaper when she gulped.

CHAPTER 53

"I DON'T WANT TO do this Gavin," Noelle finally said, as they drove down a narrow road that seemed to lead to nowhere.

He'd been driving with the eyes of a person possessed. Only this wasn't some demon that possessed Gavin, it was thoughts of killing the cannibal. He wasn't thinking clearly. Wasn't thinking clearly at all.

Gavin slammed on the brakes and hit the button to unlock the doors. "Then get the fuck out if you don't want to help me."

"Listen to me, Gav. For one second, listen to what someone else is telling you."

Her tone took Gavin by surprise. It was the meanest and loudest he'd ever heard her and stirred something in him. He shifted in his seat, and said, "What? What do you have to say?"

"You have no idea where this road leads," she said, pointing to the greenery ahead of them that looked like the rest of the woods they'd been dealing with. "You're gonna get us lost—get yourself lost. Then what? Then what, Gavin? Your parents lose *two* children to these fucking woods?"

Gavin gritted his teeth. He hadn't thought of that. He looked out the windshield, hoping that by some miracle they'd see the Camp Slaughter sign—the one with the fading family—

or anything hinting that they were on the right path, but there was nothing. She was right. It was like staring at an abyss of trees and leaves. He had no idea where this dirt road led, and they were at a point where it wasn't too late to turn back.

"Brooke was right," Noelle continued, seeing he was considering what she was saying. "We need to get the police out here. This is a job for them, not us. Not us, Gav. Do it for your brother. Wayne wouldn't want you to get killed for him, would he? Turn the car around before we get lost, Gav, please."

"You're right," he said, meekly.

All they had was a fire poker and an ax and his balls of steel. If it really came down to a confrontation, would any of that make a difference against a crazed cannibal?

No, it wouldn't. As much as he didn't want to admit it, this was an awful plan that would just get them killed.

He made a U-turn on the dirt road, having to drive several feet into the grass in the woods to complete it, and then headed back to Lakewood Cabin for the second time.

From there, they would take the road they knew back to the main roads. It would be at least forty-minutes until they were in a town, and this didn't sit right with Gavin, because it was possible everyone they were leaving behind would be dead by then.

But Noelle was right. There was no better option.

Mamá's birthday was ruined, but that didn't mean the fun had to end.

Ignacio got control of himself and looked over at the new Barbie. Blood continued to come out of her wounds, with no signs of stopping. She would probably bleed to death and die without him fixing her up, but so be it.

There was too much work to do to worry about it. He had to save Mamá's special day. And the only way to do that was by killing those who'd ruined it.

Ignacio turned his attention to the old Barbie, whose back was pressed against the wall. She was looking at him with sunken eyes swimming with fear. A croak escaped between her dry, cracked, bleeding lips. Her bones could be seen through her yellowing skin. And her hair—Oh God, her hair—it was awful. Stringy, thin, and greasy.

She would have to be replaced soon.

That was OK, though. It was the beginning of summer, there would be plenty of campers around until early November. The old Barbie would be replaced well before that, but in the meantime, she would continue to be his toy.

Ignacio walked over to her and licked her cheek like it was ice cream. The skin was wet and salty from her tears.

"*Shh, shhh, shh,*" he said to her. "Okay…everything okay."

He put his arms around her and cradled her close to him like a baby.

Now, Nadine thought. Now was the time.

In a quick motion, Nadine reached behind her buttocks, grabbed the revolver, and swung her arm to aim at Varias Caras.

But he was quick to get up and jump backward, making the shot just a bit harder. Nadine pulled the trigger, but the gun was too heavy, and her hands were too weak to hold a steady aim, and she missed.

Too good to be true, Nadine thought, watching him hurtle through the air in what seemed like slow motion, but there was nothing she could do. This was it. This was the end for her. She was as sure of this as she'd ever been of anything.

Varias Caras screamed as he grabbed her throat. He smashed her head against the wall, the impact was so hard that the revolver flew out of her hands. The bones in her body seemed to all rattle at once.

He brought her forward again, still holding her by the neck, then slammed her head into the wall as hard as he could. The wall shook, a bolt flew off from the metal where the cuffs were chained to, and the back of Nadine's head cracked open.

The blood and bits of bone that stained the wall looked like raspberry pie being thrown against it. Nadine was dead, but Varias Caras had lost all control of himself. He slammed her against the wall a third time, making the mess of blood and brain matter on the wall bigger.

He got up, wiped his hands on the front of his pants, and shook his head as if he couldn't believe what he'd done. Or rather, he couldn't believe what it had come to.

In his outburst, his hearing sensitivity had gone all the way up, and he could hear a car engine out in the woods. It was about half a mile out, maybe a little more, but he knew what it was. Nothing in the natural world of the woods sounded anything like the rumbling of a vehicle's engine. It was the sound of prey to him.

Ignacio barged out of the barn, not bothering to open the door and instead bashing it open with his good shoulder.

He closed his eyes and focused his hearing to get the location of the car. The leaves the car rustled as it blew past them told Ignacio where it was and where it was heading. They were trying to get away, but they weren't far enough yet. He knew how to get ahead of them if he hurried through the woods.

Ignacio ran into the barn. He needed more than his machete (which was still hanging on his back) for this one, because he wanted there to be carnage.

These campers ruined Mamá's birthday, and they would pay for it.

He grabbed his chainsaw from the shelf and started off into the woods.

CHAPTER 54

THE ADVANTAGE OF traveling by foot was that he didn't need to stay on the cleared roadways. Ignacio cut through the trees, sprinting as fast as he could, revving the chainsaw. Meanwhile, he kept his hearing focused on the car. He could hear it whizzing through the roads. They were speeding.

Going fast, fast, fast.

But that was fine. His shortcut was faster.

A few seconds later, he emerged out of the woods on the road in front of the car. He could hear where it was coming from better now. It would only be a couple of minutes until it came around the bend he was standing in.

That was plenty of time to prepare. He found a branch on a tree that looked good enough for what he had planned and headed to it.

It was Gavin and Noelle that Ignacio was waiting for around the bend and up the incline, because Brooke Florentine was long gone. She was flooring the accelerator, with getting to safety the only thing on her mind.

Guilt of having left the others behind tried to invade her thoughts, but she didn't let it. The others had made their choices. Gavin and Noelle could have escaped with her, but instead decided to go back where the cannibal was. Where gunshots had been heard.

A stupid decision that they must've known could (*would*, Brooke thought) cost them their lives. And if it did, that had nothing to do with Brooke.

She'd stop at the first store she saw and use their phone to call the police, to let them know that her friends were in the woods with a maniac trying to kill them. She'd have to do it that way because in the madness of arguing with Noelle and Gavin and scrambling out of the cabin, she'd forgotten her cell phone.

The phone didn't matter to her as much as it once had. All that mattered was getting out of these damned woods and finding safety. The first car she'd see would look like a godsend.

The first road sign would, too, for that matter.

Gavin whipped the car around the bend so fast Noelle was sure that they were about to tip onto two tires. She let out a shriek, but it was nothing in comparison to the scream that came out of her next.

The Honda went up the hill at the end of the bend, and there he was. The masked cannibal stood on top of a boulder, waiting for them. He was holding a hefty tree branch like a spear, and it was aimed right at the car.

"GAVIN! STOP THE CAR! STOP THE CAR!" Noelle screamed at the top of her lungs.

Gavin had seen him at the same time she had and was already slamming on the brakes. The brakes screeched as the tires kicked up dirt. The car started sliding to the right, but also kept going forward.

Varias Caras threw the tree branch, pointed end first, right at the windshield. It went through the glass, exploding shards everywhere, but it missed hitting either of them. Instead, it went between their seats and went through the car until getting lodged in the backseat.

The impact of the tree branch made the car spin out of Gavin's control. They both screamed as the car went around and around like a fucked-up version of the Tilt-O-Whirl.

It spun three full circles, before the car finally smashed into a tree on the side of the road.

Her vision was blurry. Her ears were ringing. Noelle had taken the brunt of the impact since the car struck the tree on the passenger side. Her right arm was broken in several places, her head felt heavy. She wanted so badly to go to sleep.

But then she blinked, and saw Rachel appear on the hood of the car. Her little sister sat cross-legged on the crumpled-up hood, surrounded by gray smoke billowing out from the busted engine. There was a sheen to her skin, like she was glowing, and she was whole, with no wounds.

"You just going to sit there, big sister? Or are you going to help him?" Rachel said.

She was pointing at the driver seat, where a semi-conscious Gavin was feeling around for the door handle to get out of the car. There was a large shard of glass sticking out from one of his shoulders, and his shirt was covered in blood, but the worst damage he sustained had been when his head bounced off the steering wheel on impact.

"It's just like our car accident," Noelle said to her sister.

Rachel nodded. "Here's your chance, Noelle. To make things right for yourself. To finally rid yourself of the guilt."

"I—I can hardly feel my body, Rach… I don't know if I have the energy…"

"Grab my hand," Rachel said, sticking her arm out. "I can only do this once, before I have to go."

"What?"

"Grab my hand, Noelle." Rachel reached her hand through the windshield.

Not just through one of holes where glass was missing, Rachel's hand went through even the shards still clinging to the frame.

Noelle grabbed her hand. It was warm—warmer than humanly possible—and in that instance realized why her sister didn't appear damaged like her usual hallucinations. Because this wasn't a hallucination.

This actually was Rachel. It was her sister's ghost. These woods were haunted, and they'd brought Rachel's ghost to come help her.

Noelle crawled through the windshield. The shards of glass still stuck to the car were like teeth in a shark's mouth, and they cut her open in several places as Rachel pulled her onto the hood.

The smoke was thick, and she coughed, but held her composure. Rachel pointed into the car, where the ax was resting on the dashboard. It must've slipped out of Noelle's hands on the impact of the crash and landed there.

"Don't forget that," Rachel said.

Noelle reached through the windshield and grabbed the weapon. She turned to thank Rachel, but she was gone.

Gavin unlocked the car door, rolled out of it, and fell to the ground. His back struck a big rock laying on the ground, but he didn't care. Other parts of his body hurt worse.

He laid there for a moment, in a daze, but as his mind started to regroup, he remembered where he was and what was happening.

He sat up, and saw the cannibal tearing across the dirt road. He held the chainsaw over his head, ready to bring it down.

Gavin reached into his shorts and pulled out the steak knife he'd grabbed from the kitchen. At the time, it'd seemed like a good idea, but with the danger now in front of him, he realized he would've been as good with a butter knife.

Using the side of the car for support, he got to his feet, and turned around in time to see the cannibal swinging the chainsaw down at him.

Gavin watched the chain spinning around the blade in a mesmerized state. He never thought that accepting death would be so calming.

Putting her hips into the motion, Noelle swung the ax as hard as she could with her good arm. The ax went into Varias Caras' chest, and the surprise of the attack took him off balance. He stumbled backward, tripped on his own two feet and fell on his ass. The chainsaw flew out of his grip.

"We have to go!" Noelle screamed, and pulled Gavin by the collar of his shirt, but he didn't move.

His head had cleared, and he saw the cannibal was on the ground trying to pull the ax out of his chest.

This was his moment to strike.

Gavin shook his head at Noelle, and picked up the rock he'd fallen on when he got out of the car. It was about the size of a football, and heavy enough to do damage.

Gavin positioned the rock so the most jagged side of it was sticking out, and then ran toward the cannibal, and leapt into the air. He smashed the rock against the side of his head.

Ignacio slumped forward; the back of his head exposed.

He was badly hurt. No way Gavin was going to let this opportunity go.

This one was for Wayne.

He brought the rock down as hard as he could on the cannibal's head. There was a thud, like a tennis ball striking a brick wall, and then Varias Caras fell sideways.

Noelle grabbed Gavin by his shirt again and pulled him. He didn't know what she was saying because his mind was processing a million thoughts, but he knew she was telling him to run.

And as much as he wanted to kill him, as much as it would have been satisfying to pulverize his skull, he knew she was right. There was no promise this monster wasn't going to get up, grab one of the weapons, and take their heads off.

Besides, she'd come back to save his sorry ass. He owed her.

Gavin pulled Noelle's hand off his shirt and squeezed it. Then, together, they ran into the woods as fast as their damaged bodies would let them.

CHAPTER 55

IGNACIO SAT UP. The back of his head was throbbing, pounding, like someone was knocking on the inside of his skull.

The chainsaw laid a few feet from him, the motor slowed down to a purr and the chain was coming to a stop.

Stupid brain…stupid brain, he scolded himself, because he couldn't remember what happened.

He blinked and shook his head in frustration. He still couldn't remember.

Then he saw the car. The passenger side was smooshed into the trunk of a massive oak tree that had held strong against the crash. The tree branch he'd thrown was sticking out of the middle of the windshield.

He remembered now.

He'd tried fighting them but lost. That's why his head hurt. That's why he was bleeding.

But maybe… Maybe he could still find them.

Ignacio tried focusing his hearing, but it didn't work. He couldn't hear far away anymore. The knocks to his head must have done something to his brain. Made it stupider.

He walked over to the chainsaw and picked it up as it went dead silent. The tranquility of the woods returned and surrounded him.

Mamá's birthday was ruined. Both of his Barbies were dead—unless by some miracle the new one was alive, but he wasn't counting on that because he hadn't treated her wounds. She'd probably bled to death by now. And two of his prey had gotten away. They would tell on him. The police might believe them, too, because they were cut up and hurt.

This wasn't how things were supposed to go.

Stupid Ignacio. You ruin everything. He started back into the woods.

He stopped at the front of the wrecked car and stared at it for a good while. This had been too much for him. He should've left those campers alone, but the desire for the new Barbie had gotten the best of him.

All because she looked like Mamá. And in an awful twist, he'd ruined Mamá's special day trying to find a girl to replace the missing part of his heart. The one that was lost when those thieves had killed her in cold blood.

Tears came down his eyes as he walked back to the farmhouse, shoulders slumped in defeat.

They couldn't run anymore. There was no more energy left in them, they'd lost too much blood. They both fell onto a dirt road that was a little under half a mile from where they fought the cannibal. Not that either of them knew how far they'd gone. They just knew they couldn't go any further. This was where they would die or be rescued. Silently, they'd both made up their minds about that.

Gavin and Noelle were laying down on their stomachs, their hands had let go of the others when they fell, but their outstretched fingers were inches away from touching.

Noelle turned her head to face Gavin. "Are—are you okay?"

Gavin shook his head. "Are you?"

"Nope," she said.

"Do you think any of the others survived?" Gavin asked her.

"No," she said, and to her surprise a dry chuckle escaped between her lips. "I… I'm not even sure we survived."

With the last of his energy, Gavin curled his lips into a smile. Then, he was out.

Noelle closed her eyes, and shortly after, she went unconscious, too.

"Dad! Stop the truck!" Benji shouted.

Bill Hutcherson was on his cellphone, trying to drive and figure out how to change the background image of his new iPhone X at the same time, to prove to his son his old man still had it. He looked up from the screen when he heard his son shouting and saw the two people lying in the middle of the road.

"Holy smokes!" Bill yelled as he slammed the brakes and veered his truck off to the shoulder.

Everything in the car, including the coins in the cupholders and the American flag air freshener hanging on the rearview mirror, moved to the right with the change in direction.

The truck stopped at the side of the road, kicking up clumps of grass and dirt behind its tires. Bill took his camo hat off his head and wiped his brow with it. That was a close call. He would've run the two poor things over if Benji weren't with him.

While his dad was catching his breath from nearly turning the two people laying in the street into roadkill, Benji slid out of the car.

"Grab one of the rifles, boy!" Bill shouted after him, then undid his seatbelt and climbed out the car.

Benji retrieved one of the rifles they had on the bed of the truck and approached the bodies. They were both disheveled and covered in blood and he thought that was a bone sticking out of one of the girl's arms. Benji had seen a kid break his arm after falling out of a tree last year. This was nothing new to him, so he managed to keep his cool.

He scanned the area for any hints of what might've happened to them, but there were none. Just trees and bushes and a chipmunk scurrying on the ground a few yards away. Benji drew closer, then crouched down and grabbed the guy's wrist. There was a pulse. He grabbed the girl's good arm next, and also felt a pulse.

"Dad!" he said as his old man approached him with a rifle of his own. "They're alive, Dad!"

Bill crouched down over the bodies, and Benji moved away to give him more space. He checked them for life just as his son had done.

"Well, I'll be damned," he said, glad that the two were alive—but first and foremost he was proud of his boy for knowing what to do in this situation.

"Come on, Benj. Help me load 'em into the truck. It'll be no different than how we carry the deer."

Benji grabbed Gavin's legs, while Bill hauled him up by the arms. On a deer, Bill would've been pulling by the front legs, but it was the same idea. Bill counted to three, then lifted him up and they carried him to the back of the truck.

Next, they picked Noelle up. It was a little trickier because of her broken arm, but Bill pressed his hip against her shoulder to bear some of the weight that way. A minute or so after they found them, they were both loaded into the back of the truck, still unconscious.

Billy and Benji climbed back into their seats. They had been on their way to fish at a remote river that was only a mile and a half away from here, but it seemed God had changed their plans.

Billy made a U-turn on the dirt road and drove the truck toward town to take their knocked-out passengers to the hospital.

"What a strange day, huh, Dad?" Benji said.

"Yeah," Bill responded. "Wonder what happened to 'em?"

"Maybe a bear?" Benji offered.

"Maybe, son. Maybe."

They didn't say another word to each other until they got to the hospital. The whole time, though, they speculated what could've happened to them.

Out here, the possibilities were endless.

Gavin was hallucinating. Had to be. There was no way he was on a stretcher right now, being carried through the doors of a hospital. This was all just an illusion his mind was creating to make it easier to accept death.

Yeah, that had to be it. In reality, he was still laying somewhere in the woods. The cannibal with the chainsaw would come get him any second. Chop him up and turn him into porkchops or bacon or whatever sick shit he did with the people he killed. Maybe he fucked them.

He hoped he wouldn't do that to Noelle. She didn't deserve it.

The thought of her made him lift his head up.

"Lie down, young man. Stay calm. You're alright now." One of the medics carrying the stretcher, a man with a full gray head of hair, spoke to him gently. "You're OK now, son. Take it easy."

"Noelle…" Gavin said, letting his head drop back down because it was too heavy to hold up.

"The girl is fine, sweetie." This came from the other side of the stretcher, from a heavyset black woman with a slight southern accent. "Ya'll are both gonna be just fine."

And Gavin believed her. He believed that voice that was smooth and sweet as honey. Even though his whole body ached, and the wounds underneath the thick layer of bandages pulsed in throbbing pain, Gavin believed her.

He closed his eyes and fell asleep in peace, knowing the nightmare was over.

EPILOGUE

After treating his wounds, Ignacio spent the day collecting the bodies of people he'd killed. The old man hanging from the tree, the scrawny kid bent in half in the woods, the blue-haired guy back at Lakewood Cabin (and the two heads), and finally the decapitated kid at the campsite.

He brought them to the barn where the three dead women were. He cut Mamá's lookalike's face off with a carving knife and folded it up in Saran paper he got from the farmhouse. He put her face in his pocket for later.

The other bodies he cut up for the parts he could use for meals—the thighs, the backs, the shoulders, the bellies and put them in plastic bags—then stacked the remains of the corpses into a pile in the middle of the barn.

Next, he went to the farmhouse where he took out all of his necessities and treasured items and loaded them into the car; the candles, the Jesus statue, his cooking dishes, his clothes, his boots, his masks, his machete, and of course the stick with Mamá's head on it.

He took the gallons of gasoline he had stocked up for the car, poured it all over the farmhouse, then lit a match and threw it inside. He took some of the remaining gas over to the barn and did the same thing.

Both buildings would burn down. Maybe they'd cause a forest fire. Maybe they'd burn miles and miles of the place he used to call home. But he didn't care. He'd be long gone from here by then.

And as long as he had his Mamá's head, anywhere could be home for Ignacio.

It was around six PM when reports of people seeing smoke from the highway came in, and past midnight by the time the firefighters put the last of the flames out. The fire had spread from the barn all the way through the entire camp by means of dry brush and grass and trees, so when the firetrucks arrived on the scene, the campgrounds were up in a blaze.

Around the time the firefighters were wrapping things up, Gavin and Noelle were talking to the police. When they arrived at the location to investigate what the two kids had told them, the only things left were burned trees, charred husks of wood, and ashes that were soaked wet from the firetruck's hoses, but nothing that would lead them to the person who murdered the campers.

All the officials had read the sign—the only thing that hadn't been engulfed in flames—when they drove to the site:

CAMP SLAUGHTER

And all of them, independently of each other, thought it was a good thing the place had burned down. There was something strange about it, but they couldn't quite put it into words. Just a feeling. Like they were being watched from the shadows. None of them spoke about it to the others, worried they'd sound foolish.

Besides, it wasn't like they were going to catch the murderer anyway. Even with all the blood they found back at Lakewood Cabin, there wasn't much of a chance they'd catch the culprit. Out here, this deep in the woods, he could've been hiding anywhere.

AFTERWORD

There are probably a lot of questions in your mind right now. Like, what happened to the survivors when they got back home? Do Brooke, Noelle, and Gavin ever talk to each other again? Will Varias Caras continue to kill?

I can't answer these questions, because I don't really know. But there's a reason I didn't write "the end" at the conclusion of this story. This is only part one.

Varias Caras will return… There's more to his legend. But for now, that's all I'll say.

Thanks for reading!

-S. Gomez

ACKNOWLEDGEMENTS

As always, I must thank Laura and Derrick first. They read the first draft of this novel and gave me valuable feedback and notes. I would lose my mind without your help and support.

Oh, and sorry to Laura for this story terrifying you so much that you had to run across your work parking lot and lock your car doors in a panic. I hope you don't think about this book on one of your camping trips.

A big thank you to subscribers of the Patreon: Jon, Laura, Derrick, Cosmo, and Nikki V. Your support makes a world of difference at keeping this dream alive.

And thanks to all the readers who've reached out to me on social media with praise. It makes the hours of isolation writing and editing these stories not feel so lonely.

ABOUT THE AUTHOR

Born in Mexico but raised in the United States, Sergio Gomez lives in Philadelphia with his family. He enjoys reading, martial arts, cooking, but most of all writing. His favorite superhero is either Batman or Hellboy depending on the day. Sergio has written two other novels and a short-story collection.

You can follow him on social media:
Instagram: @sergiopgomez
Twitter: @SergioP_Gomez
Facebook.com/AuthorSergioGomez
Or support him at **Patreon.com/SergioGomez**